Some reviews of Jiggy

The Poltergoo
Shortlisted for the Blue Pete...
"A laugh a minute. I couldn't stop turning the pages!"
Caroline, age 12

"A mix of sitcom farce and hardboiled American detective novel.
The book's climax – the reburial of a goose with a restless
spirit – features a hilarious sequence in a ladies toilet."
Michael Thorn, *Times Educational Supplement*

The Killer Underpants
Winner of the Stockton Children's Book of the Year Award
"...the funniest book I've ever read."
Teen Titles

"Very funny, pretty rude, and sometimes revolting!"
Lorraine Orman, *Story-Go-Round*

The Toilet of Doom
"Fast, furious and full of good humour."
National Literacy Association

Maggot Pie
"Will have you squirming with horror and delight!"
Ottakars 8-12 Book of the Month

"Funny, wacky and lively."
cool-reads.co.uk

The Snottle
"Awesome!"
5 Star Amazon review by Charlie, age 10

Nudie Dudie
Winner of the Doncaster Children's Book Award
Winner of the Solihull Children's Book Award
Highly Commended for the Sheffield Children's Book Award
"Fantastic! ...will make you giggle and laugh till it hurts
you so bad you start jumping up and down."
5 Star Amazon review by Kaz, age 13

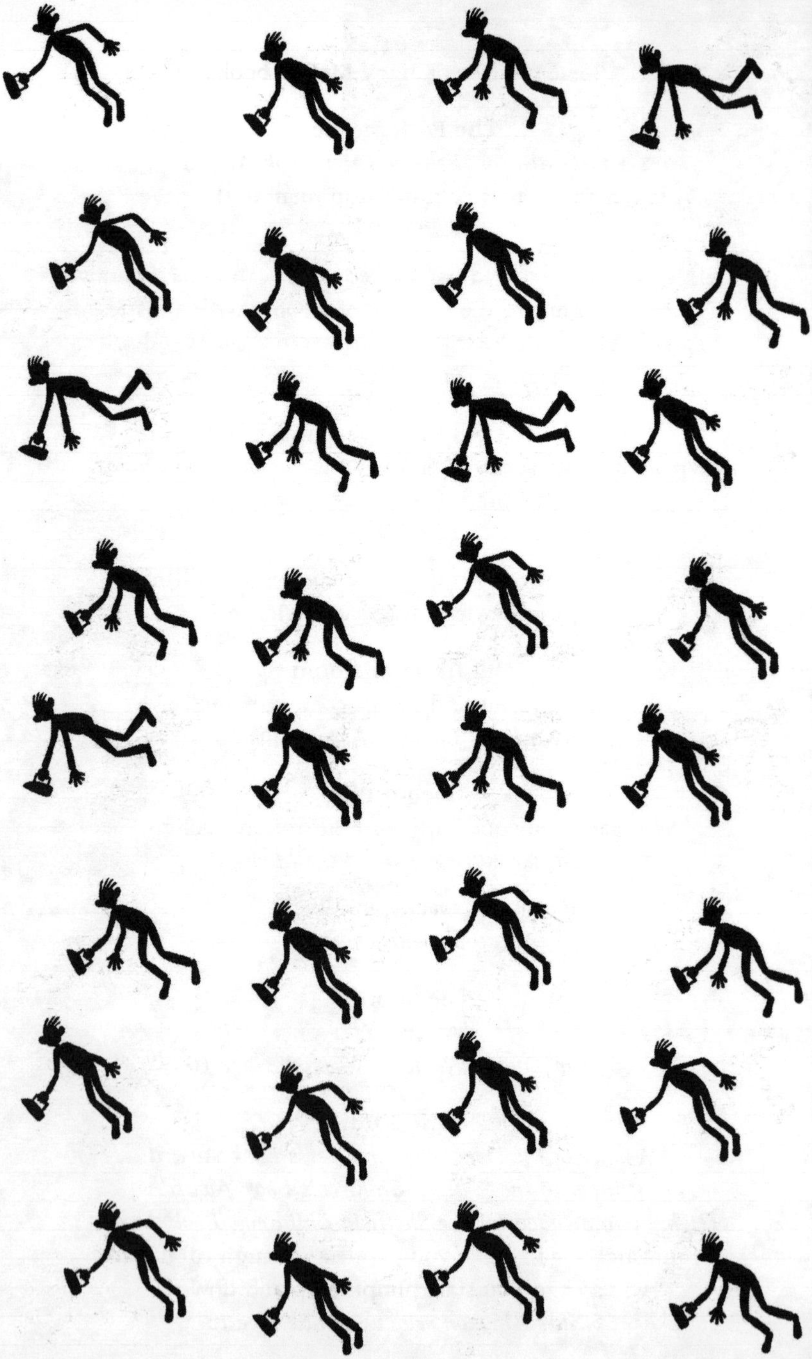

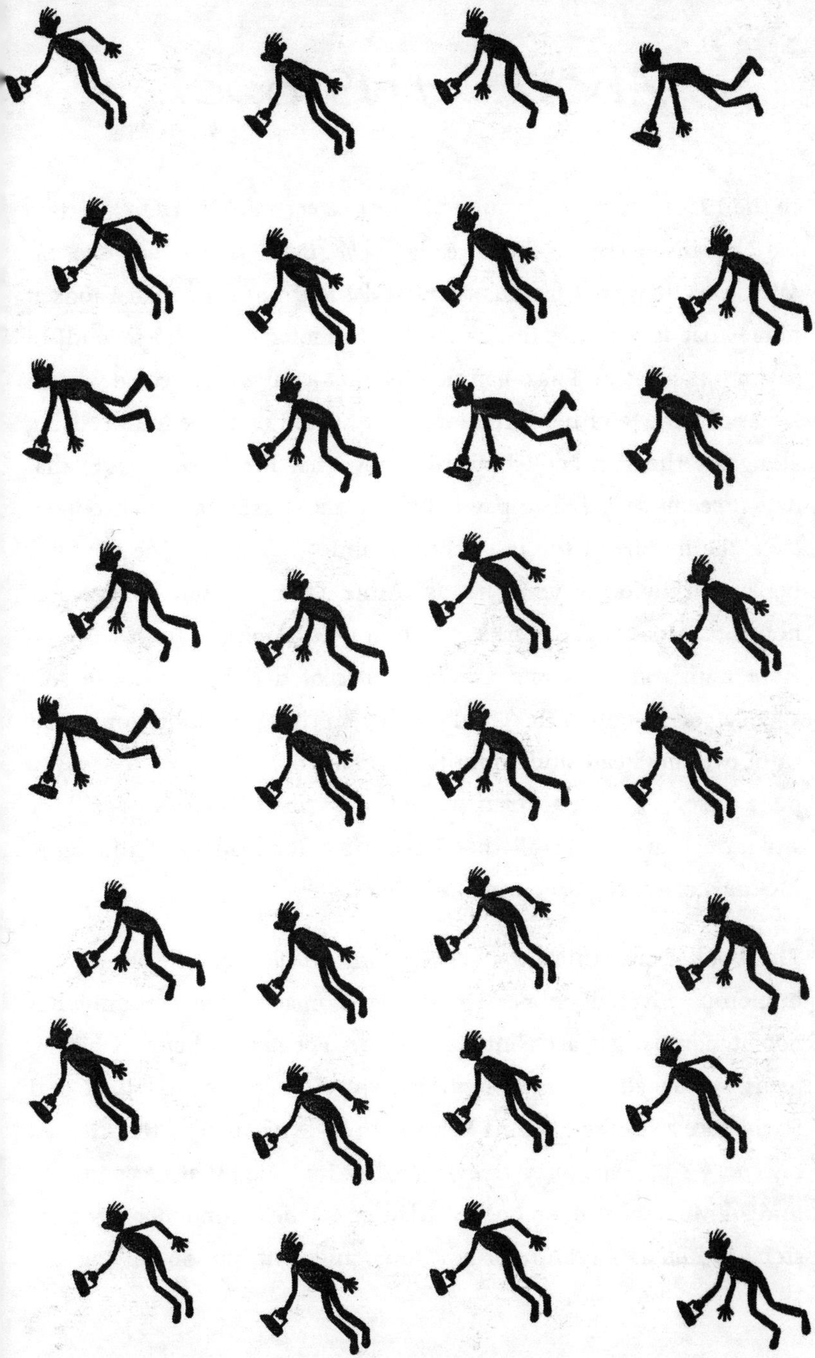

About this book

In the 1950s, a frequent young visitor to a certain library in a certain park, I discovered a book called *The Lion, the Witch and the Wardrobe*. It wasn't famous then, and I had no idea when I took it home that it was the first (though chronologically the second) of seven linked titles. I also had no idea that a day would come when a series of mine (a rather different series) would often be found sitting alongside them in bookshops. But now that I'm knee-deep in that day, it seems only fair to pay tribute to those captivating chronicles from the middle of the last century, and this I have done with the book you hold in your hands. Mine is not a slavish homage, however. Most of the works of fiction that I look fondly back upon were high romances and thrilling tales of derring-do whose sole agenda was to entertain. Thinly-veiled spiritual regurgitations went right over my head, and mightily glad I am of it. All I wanted was to be amused, gripped, transported to someone else's world or situation – and that's all that I seek to offer readers of the Jiggy McCue stories. No Deep Meanings here!

The book from which the present one sneaks its title was not a humorous novel, of course. Exciting, yes, imaginative, certainly, but not humorous. It wasn't intended to be. For laughs before I hit my teens, I turned to Anthony Buckeridge's tales of Jennings and Darbishire at Linbury Court School – a style of humour that tickled my every rib. Some forty-five years after I decided that I was too old to read Mr Buckeridge's books, I dedicated the second Jiggy McCue story to him as a gesture of gratitude, and sent him one of the few hardback copies that had been printed. Being in a position to do this was gratifying enough, but it was nothing to what happened a few evenings later. In a rather tetchy mood when the phone rang that night, I grabbed the receiver, barked 'Yes!', heard a gentle voice saying, 'Hello, Anthony Buckeridge here...', and suddenly I was eleven again, stammering inarticulately to an 88 year old author I'd revered when I was Jiggy's age.

It pleases me to hope that many years from the one in which *The Iron, the Switch and the Broom Cupboard* first found its way into bookshops and libraries, the odd Golden Oldie will look back on it with a smile similar to my own when I think of my first encounters with Jennings, Darbishire and *The Chronicles of Narnia*. Maybe you'll be one of those Golden Oldies. It will be a long time before you know, of course. Sadly I never will, but that's the thing about time: it moves on. Authors too.

Michael Lawrence

Each Jiggy book is a story on its own right, but if you would like to read them in the order in which they were written, it is:

The Poltergoose, The Killer Underpants
The Toilet of Doom, Maggot Pie
The Snottle, Nudie Dudie
Neville the Devil, Ryan's Brain,
The Iron, the Switch and The Broom Cupboard

ONE FOR ALL AND ALL FOR LUNCH!
Visit Michael at his website: www.wordybug.com

The Iron, the Switch and the Broom Cupboard

ORCHARD BOOKS
338 Euston Road, London NW1 3BH
Orchard Books Australia
Level 17/207 Kent Street, Sydney, NSW 2000
ISBN 978 1 84616 471 2
A Paperback Original
First published in 2007 by Orchard Books
Text © Michael Lawrence 2007
Illustrations © Ellis Nadler 2007
A CIP catalogue record for this book is available from the British Library
3 5 7 9 10 8 6 4
Printed in Great Britain

Orchard Books is a division of Hachette Children's Books
www.orchardbooks.co.uk

A JIGGY McCUE STORY

The Iron, the Switch and the Broom Cupboard

Michael Lawrence

ORCHARD BOOKS

*I would like to dedicate this book to
Penny Morris, long-suffering editor of it and
a variety of others that we've somehow managed
to produce between lively lunches, strolls in
literary gardens, and casual forays
into days gone by.*

Chapter one

I was woken by the jolly sound of my mother throwing up in the bathroom. Good job too. That she was throwing up in the bathroom, I mean. It would have taken her ages to get it out of the carpet on the landing. Naturally, I would have preferred to be woken by the tweet-tweet of dear little birdies in the trees that aren't outside my window, but I never get any say in these things.

'Is it me?' I asked, sliding out of bed and peeking round my bedroom door as she staggered out to the landing.

'Is what you?' she gurgled.

'Well, you're always saying I make you sick…'

She smiled feebly – 'Remind me to avoid prawn curries' – and tottered downstairs.

Before I go any further I'd better tell you my name. It's McCue, Jiggy McCue, double-o-nothing, stirred, not shaken. You might know that already. If you don't know it already, it's still Jiggy McCue.

That's Jiggy, not Ziggy or Biggy or Piggy, or Wuggy or Muggy or Buggy – and *definitely* not Juggy. You have to get that straight because of the stuff I'm going to tell you about.*

Now that I think of it, there are one or two other things I ought to get out of the way first. Here they are. I go to a school called Ranting Lane and live with my parents and cat (Mel, Peg and Stallone) in a house called *The Dorks* (yes, really) on a housing development called the Brook Farm Estate, which was built on what used to be a farm (Brook Farm). We live on the cheapo side. The really terrific houses, the ones with double garages and designer poodles and columns holding up the porches, are over on Hillary Clinton Walk, Hannibal Lector Way, and a few other streets named after someone's heroes. The not-so-upmarket streets on our side have names like Crack End and Snit Close. *The Dorks* has three bedrooms and two toilets, though we only use two of the bedrooms. My next-door neighbour is a cement-head from my class called Eejit Atkins, and just across the road is the house where Pete Garrett and Angie Mint live. Pete and Angie are my best buds. We call ourselves the Three Musketeers and

---

* Actually my real first name's Joseph, but the only people who use it are Golden Oldie teachers you can't educate. Jiggy's been a sort of nickname since I was knee-high to our garden gnome. I got it because I have this complete inability to keep still when I'm agitated or upset or scared, which means I'm as jumpy as two frogs on a bed of nails quite a lot of the time.

we're a sort of gang. Not a bad gang, we don't trip up old ladies and stuff, but when there's three of you and you hang together you have to call yourselves something.

I'd better start by telling you what happened the evening before the morning my mother chucked up in the bathroom and woke me so thoughtlessly. I was working on the Musketeer Rule Book in my room. It was a little red notebook I'd bought out of my pathetic excuse for pocket money. On the cover I'd printed our heroic battle-cry, 'One for all and all for lunch', and inside I'd written the rules that I'd been laying out for a year. It's hard work dreaming up rules, but I was already up to Rule Four, which was…

Rule 4: Musketeers must not hug (specially one another).

This was mainly for Angie. Angie's a female, but she's always saying it's not her fault. She's more boy than Pete and me put together most of the time, even though she doesn't have our dangly bits, but she forgets herself occasionally and comes over all soppy and flings her arms round you. Let me tell you, it's no fun inside a Mint bear-hug.

'Jiggy!'

That was my mum, calling from downstairs. She's always doing that, calling me from some part of the house I'm not in. Sometimes we're in the same room together and she hardly speaks, then she goes out and shouts for me, and I answer, and she says 'Pardon me?' and I repeat myself, and she says, 'Will you come here please?' and I sigh, and heave myself out of my chair or off my bed, and go to wherever she is, and she says something like, 'Hold the other end of this sheet,' like it's really urgent. There's quite a lot I don't get about my mother. Her whole generation in fact. The Golden Oldie universe is fifteen-point-four light years away from mine.

'Jiggy!'

'What?'

'Will you come down here please?'

'What for?'

'Because I'm asking you to.'

I tutted and passed through my bedroom door (which was open, I'm not a flaming ghost) and went out to the landing. I looked down the stairs. Mum wasn't there any more, which meant I couldn't interrogate her further without trudging down.

Trudge, trudge, trudge.

'Where are you?' I yell from the bottom (of the stairs).

'Who?' Dad yells back from the living room, where he's watching something sporty on TV as usual.

'Not you!' I yell back.

'I'm in the kitchen!' yells Mum.

I go into the kitchen. My mother is standing there with her ironing board.

'What?' I say.

'Will you stop saying "What?",' she says.

'I'll stop saying what if you stop calling me.'

'I'm calling you because I want to show you how to iron.'

'What?'

'I'm going to show you how to iron.'

'What?'

'Clothes. It's about time you learnt.'

'Why?' I said.

'Because if anything happened to me, you wouldn't know what to do.'

'I would. I'd go for the wrinkled look. What brought this on?'

'What brought it on is that I have so much ironing to do all the time, and get no help from you or your father.'

'Why would you? Ironing is women's work, well-known fact since the dawn of Men's Lib.'

'Jiggy, this is the twenty-first century,' Mum says.

'And this is Wednesday,' I reply.

She frowns. 'What's that got to do with anything?'

I frown back. 'Haven't a clue. Can I go now?'

'No. You'll stay here and learn to iron.'

'Mother,' I said. 'I have homework.'

'Yes,' she said. 'You do,' she said. '*This* homework. Come round here.'

I went round there. I always do as I'm told when I run out of excuses or Mum gets bossy.

Now I'm going to tell you something about ironing. What I'm going to tell you is that it isn't as easy as it looks, specially when the point of the iron gets stuck in the gusset of a pair of underpants. A handkerchief would have been easier. I suggested this, but Mum said anyone could iron a handkerchief, which was why I wasn't.

'But why underpants?' I enquired.

'Underpants are just the start,' she replied. 'You take it for granted when you open your drawer and see them lying there neatly pressed. Well, now you're going to learn how they get that way.'

'Mum.'

'What?'

'It doesn't matter to me if my underpants aren't neatly pressed.'

'Well, it should.'

'Well, it doesn't. It wouldn't matter to me if they were as wrinkled as a pair of prunes. I don't care if my underpants are pressed, tied in a bow, or have tyre marks. No one in their right mind *would* care.'

'I care,' said Mum.

'My point exactly,' I said.

'Whatever you say, Jiggy, whether you like it or not, from now on you're pressing your own underpants.'

'These aren't my underpants.'

'No, they're your father's. We're using his things to practice on. If you make a mess of your dad's clothes he won't notice. He has no pride *whatever* in his appearance.'

'Well nor do I.'

'No, but just in case you develop some eventually I'm going to show you how to look smart. You'll thank me one day.'

'I'll visit the Home specially,' I said.

It wasn't just underpants either. She also tried to show me how to iron T-shirts, and shirts that weren't teed, and pyjamas, and quite a few other things. I grumbled a bit more, naturally, but after a while it got kind of interesting. Kind of a challenge to make everything smooth. I felt like I'd failed when I made a crease where there wasn't one before.

Dad strolled in while I was struggling with one of his shirt collars. 'This I do not believe,' he said, stopping in his tracks and grabbing the door to support himself.

I scowled at him so he wouldn't know it wasn't as bad as it looked. 'You don't have to believe it. I'm going to wake up in a minute and tell you all about it. Then we can both crack up.'

'I'm teaching your son to appreciate the things that are done for him,' Mum explained.

'You don't plan on teaching me too, do you?'

said Dad, worried.

'Oh no, you're past saving. Lost cause, you.'

'Whew,' he said, and scooted back to the telly.

As it happened, my mother did me a favour, showing me how to iron. Why was that a favour? Because of what was coming, that's why. If you want to hear what that was, stick around. If you don't, go and press someone's underpants. And watch that gusset!

Chapter Two

Thursday. The morning I was woken from my sweet dreams by my old dear throwing up in the bathroom. I was down in the kitchen gulping my cereal when I heard the post drop through the letterbox.[1] I went out to the hall and picked the envelopes up from the mat, hoping there was one for me.[2] There wasn't, never is, but I live in hope. I'm thinking of sending myself a letter so I'll have one to open like everyone else. The reason I haven't done that so far is that it wouldn't be much of a surprise, even if I disguised the handwriting. There were three envelopes today, including a couple of long ones with windows, which Dad snatched off me only to drop them right away like they were on fire.

'Bills!' he snarled. 'Why do I only ever get *bills*?'

'Look on the bright side,' I said. 'Bill probably gets yours.'

There was also one for Mum, with the name of the

---

[1] Post as in letters, not a long bit of wood.

[2] Envelope, not mat.

local hospital in small print in the top left-hand corner. When she came down she opened it and read the page inside.

'Monday afternoon,' she said to Dad.

'Bit short-notice,' he replied.

'Has to be, I suppose.'

'I'll take the day off,' he said.

'You don't have to, I can still drive.'

'Give up an excuse for not going to work? No chance.'

'You don't have to take the whole day. The appointment's not till two.'

'Oh, it's hardly worth going in just for the morning.'

'You know, Mel, your dedication to work is like Jiggy's to school.'

'What's going on?' I asked them.

Mum glanced at me. 'Going on?'

'This hospital appointment.'

'I'm just having something checked,' she said, slotting the letter back in the envelope and dropping it in the shoulder bag she wears to work.

'Having what checked?'

'Don't go on, Jiggy, it's nothing, here's your lunch

box, you'll find some sardine-and-tomato paste sandwiches in there.'

'Sardine-and-tomato paste sandwiches?'

'And some new-flavour crisps I came across in SmartSave.'

'Mum. I don't like sardine-and-tomato paste sandwiches.'

'Oh, you're always saying that.'

'Yes,' I said. 'I am,' I said. 'And guess why,' I said. 'BECAUSE I DON'T LIKE THEM!'

'There's no need to shout,' she said, and left the kitchen, which meant I'd still be getting sardine-and-tomato paste sandwiches when I'm forty-three. I don't know what you have to do to get through to Golden Oldies, I really don't.

I met Angie and Pete outside as usual and we set off with lead in our socks like we do most school mornings. Halfway along the street, Angie shuddered. I asked her why.

'I just walked on the paving stone Dawn Overton was mugged on.'

'How do you know it was that one?'

'She showed me.'

'How does she remember the exact paving stone?'

'There's still a mark – look.'

Dawn Overton and her mother Mrs Overton (Janet) are my next-door neighbours on the side that doesn't contain the Atkins family. Dawn's a nurse.* Not long ago she and her mum got a dog, a big hairy beast called Charlie Farnsbarns. Every evening that it's not raining, Mrs Overton kicks Charlie F into the back garden and says, so loudly the whole estate can hear without straining, 'Do your business, Charlie Farnsbarns!' She says this over and over – 'Do your business, Charlie Farnsbarns! Do your business, Charlie Farnsbarns!' – until the critter's done it. Mum and Dad and I realised what a regular event this was on a few evenings in the summer when we had tea in the back garden, just over the fence from the Overtons'. When you're tucking into something that could be anything, like most of the food my mother dishes up, one thing you don't want to hear over the fence, repeated with every swallow, is, 'Do your business, Charlie Farnsbarns!' because you know what that business is and it's hard not to think of the dog doing it.

Anyway. The night Dawn Overton was mugged, Charlie Farnsbarns had got out of their front gate,

* The same Dawn Overton who got a panoramic view of my bare behind in *Nudie Dudie* after it was attacked by a seagull.

23

mooched along a bit, and done his business on the pavement for a change. Mrs Overton came looking for him, found him, ordered him back into the garden, and Dawn went out to shovel the doggy biz into a small carrier bag. She'd just finished and straightened up when a boy on a mountain bike snatched the bag and rode off with it.

'Wonder what he said when he opened the bag?' Pete said.

'My guess is he described the contents in a single word not beginning with J,' said Angie.

'J?' I said.

'Joy,' she snapped. 'Not everything's about you, you know.'

'Wotcher, you free!' bawled a croaky little voice behind us.

We groaned. Eejit Atkins. Eejit talks like no one else except his brother Jolyon, Sir Hooligan of the Brook Farm Estate. No one else we know speaks like those two, including their parents. Mystery where they got it from as they grew up in the same streets as the rest of us and have been to the same school as us. Atkins-speak is kind of like measles. After a minute with Eejit or being sworn at by Jolyon, you're talking like them yourself, and then your mother tells you off like it's your fault. Even if he didn't talk that way Eejit wouldn't be the brightest candle on the cake, but I sometimes get the idea that he works at it because in his tiny mind he thinks it's cool to be a moron.

'Lo, Eejit,' I said wearily.

'Get lost, Atkins,' said Pete. Pete's not as kind to the mentally challenged as I am.

'I wuz talkin' ta me bruvver yesterdy,' Eejit said, frowning at his feet as he tried to get them to walk in step with ours. When he managed it, Pete did a little skip and got straight out of step.

'Musta bin excitin',' said Angie, dropping into Atkins-speak right away.

'Yer,' said Eejit.

And that seemed to be it.

Fifteen skippy steps on, absolutely stuffed with curiosity, I said, 'Wot wuz ya talkin' abaat?'

'Oo?' said Atkins.

'You an' Jolyon.'

'When?'

'Yesterdy.'

He shrugged. 'Search me.'

'Well why'd ya menshun it?'

'Menshun wot?'

'That you wuz talkin' to him.'

'Talkin' to oo?'

'Yer bruvver.'

'Wuz I?'

'Said ya wuz.'

'Did I?'

'Yes. You did.'

'Oh. Right.'

And that wuz it. Fairly standard conversation with Atkins. Angie, Pete and I sighed at one another.

On the other side of the main road that separates the estate from town, Eejit spied some of his idiot buds doing kangaroo impressions round a man in a wheelchair. 'Be seein' ya!' he cried, and scooted off to join in.

Then someone else came by. Mr Rice, jogging. Mr Rice is our Pointless Exercises teacher. He used to jog to school with Miss Weeks, the Deputy Head, but she'd been off having a baby and wasn't back yet. The Sugar Ricicle is about as famous as Eejit Atkins, but not for the way he talks. He doesn't actually talk anyway, he shouts – at us kids anyway – but it's not the shouting that he's famous for either, it's for always wearing a tracksuit during school-time, on the sports field, in the gym, even on the stage in Assembly, which I think is pretty sad. And it's always a red tracksuit, maybe even the same one, year in, year out. We're not great pals, Mr Rice and me. He's always trying to get me to run faster or jump higher or kick balls into giant hairnets – things that don't even make the bottom of my list of top million things I like to do.

'Hope you three are all set for the weekend!' he boomed as he jogged by in his stupid red tracksuit.

Another three-person groan. We'd been trying not to think about the weekend, when our least favourite sporty type was taking two classes from our year on a survival course in some hills.

'Why, what happens at the weekend?' I asked innocently.

He swung round to face me, jogging backwards now, holding on to his hair like it would take off if he didn't.

'You know very well what happens at the weekend, McCue, and if you're not waiting for the bus with everyone else at seven-forty-five on

Saturday morning I'll come round and personally drag you out of your pit!'

'You won't get in,' I said. 'Our door's triple locked against strange men in red. We even block the chimney to stop Father Christmas getting into our house.'

Still jogging backwards, he gave me one of his fiercest glares.

'Watch it, lad! I've got my eye on you!'

'Hey, you're not so bad yourself, sir!'

He might have said something else if his spine hadn't slammed into a lamp-post at full jog. We hurried by, covering our sniggers while he was still bouncing off the nearest rubbish bin.

Chapter Three

Most of that Thursday was like any other Thursday during term time – so yawny our toes almost dropped off with boredom. The only slightly unusual thing occurred first thing, at Assembly, because of what one of us had done the day before in History.

We didn't have History in the usual room that day because men with smears and blobs all over their white overalls were painting it. As they were painting it the same fantastically monotonous colour as before, the only difference when they finished would be that it would stink for weeks. The usual room had a blackboard because our history teacher, Mr Hurley, was old and preferred a blackboard, but the borrowed classroom had a big whiteboard whether he liked it or not. There were a couple of other differences too. As well as its own full wad of desks and chairs, the desks and chairs from the usual history room had been stacked in there, which made it kind of hard to get from A to B, or even C to P. To give us even less space, the giant photocopier from Miss Prince's office had been wheeled in because her office and the Head's were also being painted.

Now Mr Hurley is a serious man. Serious as in seriously boring. He's short and square and thick-necked, and he always wears the same check jacket, brown trousers and maroon tie, and he doesn't seem to like us much. A smile on the Hurley features in our lessons is about as rare as a pilchard quacking, and he never makes jokes. I mean he *never* makes jokes. He also doesn't have a clue most of the time when we're jerking him around. Example. A week or two before the day I'm telling you about, he came in, coughed loudly to silence us, and wrote 'Henry VIII' on the board. Then he turned to us, waited for the last of the noise to fade, and said, 'A spot of recapping today, class, starting with the six wives of Henry the Eighth. I would like their names please.'

'Bet you would,' someone muttered.

'Henry the eighth what?' someone else asked.

'He was a *king*,' Mr H said. 'Of *England*.'

'You mean he was the eighth king of England?'

'No, I mean the eighth king called Henry.'

'The eighth king called Henry? What did he call him for, sir? And what did they talk about?'

Hurley took a deep breath and started again, speaking very slowly.

'I would like this class to tell me the names of the six wives of the eighth King Henry of England. The very wives we discussed in two periods just the other week.'

'What did he want six wives for?' someone asked. 'My dad says one's one too many.'

'Don't be silly, boy, he was married to them one at a time, not all at once. Oh, you can't have forgotten their names already. Not *all* of them.'

Silence in class.

'Anyone?' he said, glaring gloomily around.

More silence.

'Can't you at least take a *stab* at this?' he asked. 'Come on, give me some names. I only want six. Is that so hard?'

Well, put like that…

Here are the six names he got before he held his hand up to stop us.

'Kirsty.'

'Saffron.'

'Kylie.'

'Sharon.'

'Jade.'

'Bert.'

Everyone except Eejit Atkins knew these weren't right, of course, but classes as boring as Hurley's have to be juiced up somehow.

But that was another day. The Wednesday I'm coming to, the Wednesday in the temporary History room, also started with a Hurley baiting session. The class was still yelling and throwing stuff and running over the extra desks when he came in with a grin on his chops – a sight which caused everyone to freeze for at least ten seconds because chop-grinning wasn't something Hurley did, ever.

'You'll be thrilled to hear that we're going to have a history test today,' he said when we were sitting down and looking his way.

Foreheads smacked desks and a hearty chorus of 'Noooooo!' went up.

'Knew you'd be keen,' he said with something

worryingly like a giggle. 'It will be a test with a difference, however,' he went on. 'The difference being that you'll choose your own questions.'

Some of us looked at others of us with puzzled expressions. Choose our own questions?

'Do they have to be questions about history?' someone asked.

'Of course they have to be about history,' H beamed. 'This is a history *lesson*. But for every question you get right you'll receive a gobstopper.'

'You mean if one of us gets a right answer we all get a gobstopper?' someone asked.

'No, I mean that the *person* who gets a right answer will get a gobstopper.'

'That'll shut some of us up,' said Holly Gilder, glaring around. Holly never plays up in class.

'To eat out of school, or at home,' H added.

'Bad for your teeth, gobstoppers,' said Pitwell.

'Since when did you care?' said Hislop.

'I don't, I'm just saying,' Pitwell replied.

'How does choosing our own questions work?' Angie asked Mr Hurley.

'I'll tell you if you'll kindly pay attention,' he answered cheerfully.

'Sir, I've got one for you,' Pete said.

'One what?'

'A question. Why isn't your nose twelve inches long?'

'My nose?'

'BECAUSE THEN IT WOULD BE A FOOT!' chorused half the class.

'That one was doing the rounds when I was a boy,' said Mr H.

'Back in Roman Times?' someone asked, to show he knew his history.

'Though I'd have thought you'd be using centimetres these days.'

Pete shook his head. 'Doesn't work. The answer to "Why isn't your nose thirty centimetres long?" would have to be "Because then it would be thirty centimetres long". How funny is that?'

'How funny is it anyway?' I said.

'Tell you what would be funny,' said Mr Hurley. 'If, just for a change, you paid me some of that attention I asked for.'

We paid attention, sort of, mainly because looking like we were paying attention to Mr Hurley was a habit we hadn't kicked yet.

34

Things would change if he went on like this, though. Someone had to ask why he was being so nice.

'Sir?'

'Yes, Mr McCue?'

'What's with the sun-has-got-his-hat-on mood?' He looked puzzled. 'The larky behaviour,' I explained. 'The big fat grin. Not like you at all.' The big fat grin withered a smidgen. 'I mean has something happened? You get the job as Maria the singing nun or something?'

'If you must know,' he replied happily, 'I'm going on a cruise.'

'A cruise?' said Martin Skinner. 'You mean like on a boat, sir?'

'No, he means on a bike, snail-brain,' said Ryan.

'A very large boat,' said Hurley. 'Next month, for thirteen weeks. My acceptance arrived this very morning.'

'Have you told Mother?'

'My mother?'

'Mr Hubbard.' (Mother Hubbard is Head of Ranting Lane School.)

'I sought Mr Hubbard's permission for leave of

absence before applying for the position. He was all in favour.'

'Couldn't wait to get rid of you,' said Majid Aziz behind his hand.

'It won't be all pleasure, though,' Hurley said. 'I'll be there to work.'

'Scrubbing the decks?' said Neil Downey.

'Giving lectures and talks.'

'What, like you do here?' said Sami Safadi.

'Like I do here, yes, but for paying guests keen to know something of the history of the places we'll be visiting.'

'What places?'

'Well, there'll actually be several cruises, one after the other, in and around the Mediterranean. We'll be docking at Messina, Alexandria, Malta, Archenland, Dubrovnik, and many other wonderful places.'

'And you'll be talking all the way?' said Pete.

'Speaking, yes, much of it.'

'And people will stop their sunbathing to listen to you?'

'Hopefully. Though I expect that some of my talks will take place on deck, or even at the sites themselves.'

'Do you know the history of all those places then?' Milo Dakin asked, winking at me. We both knew – everyone knew except the man himself – that we were milking this for every last drop so there'd be less time for his stupid test.

'No, in all honesty I can't say I do, yet,' Hurley admitted. 'I'll have quite a bit of swatting to do.'

'Bet you will,' someone said. 'Lotta flies out there.'

'Now what do you say we get on with our test?' he asked.

Before any of us could think of a good answer to that there was a knock on the door and the Head's secretary looked in.

'Mr Hurley, would you mind if I made a few quick photocopies?'

'Of course not, Miss Prince,' he said, flashing his manky choppers at her. 'Go right ahead.'

'I won't be a minute,' she said, ignoring the class whose eagerly-awaited history test she'd interrupted.

Miss Prince is a very large lady who almost always wears black leggings and always seems to be trying to forget that kids exist. While she got to work on the copier, Mr Hurley dug into his briefcase and came up with...a pack of playing cards.

'Anyone good at shuffling?' he asked.

'Yer, me!' cried Eejit, jumping to his feet.

'Here then, please, Mr Atkins.'

And Eejit *shuffled* to the front of the class.

Mr H groaned. 'I was referring to shuffling cards,' he said.

'Cards?' said Eejit.

'These,' Hurley-Burley said, holding up the pack.

Atkins thought abaat this. 'Well, I could give 'em a go.'

He took the cards from the history man and started shuffling them. Half of them shot straight up into the air, another half shot to the floor, and half slapped him in the face. Mr Hurley asked him to kindly return to his seat. Eejit kindly did so.

'Thank you, Mr Hurley,' Miss Prince said, heading for the door with her photocopies.

'My pleasure,' he said, stooping to pick up the playing cards.

'What are the cards for, sir?' Julia Frame asked.

'These are Trivial History cards,' Hurley said, shuffling them himself. 'They contain the questions I want you to try and answer. What I'd like you all to do, in turn, is choose a card at random and answer the question that's printed on it, simple as that. And here are the prizes for those who give the right answers.' He held up a bag of gobstoppers. 'Who wants to go first?'

No one answered, even for a chance to stop their gobs.

'All right,' he said. 'Who wants to be last?'

Fifteen hands hit the ceiling.

'Tell you what,' he said, 'seeing as you're all so eager, why don't we do it in seating order? No need to get up. I'll come to you. That way we won't be deafened by a cacophony of deliberately scraped chairs.'

And that's what he did, starting at the desk nearest the door and working up that aisle and down the next, the cards fanned out in his hand for us each to choose one as he got to us. We weren't allowed to take the card, just touch the one we picked, then he read the question on it and we gave him an answer.

We got as much fun as we could out of it, but it was still quite a slog. Here's the way it went, card questions first, some of our answers second.

Question. What caused the Great Depression of 1929-1933?
Answer. Too much History homework.

Question. What were Julius Caesar's famous last words?
Answer. 'Is that a sword in your hand?'

Question. What happened at Custer's Last Stand?
Answer. Someone gave him a chair.

Question. The Ancient Greeks were very fond of myths. What is a myth?
Answer. A female moth.

Question. What was Sir Francis Drake famous for?
Answer. He circumcised the world with a 100 foot clipper.

'There's a phone call for you in the office.' This was Miss Prince, poking her unsmiling head in again.

'Thanks,' said Pete, standing up.

Miss P scowled at him. 'Mr Hurley,' she said. Pete sat down again.

Mr Hurley went to the door. 'While I'm away,' he said to us, 'perhaps one of you will carry on circulating with the cards. Julia, I think.'

'Why me?' said Julia Frame.

'Because you're a responsible person.'

'I am?' she said, like it was news to her.

He handed her the Trivial History cards. 'If anyone should actually get a question right, make a note of their name on the board please.'

'How will I know if they've got one right?' Julia asked.

'The answers are upside down on the back of the cards.'

'Are they?'

'They are. But don't let anyone see them.'

'I won't!' Julia said, instantly taking charge. Loves power, that girl.

Hurley left us. Not a very clever move, leaving us alone in a classroom without a guard, but teachers never learn. Julia showed the backs of the cards to one of the girls, but even before the girl picked one, things were being thrown about, boys were making rude noises, and the spare desks were being moved into the aisles. While all this was going on, Harry Potter went to the photocopier Miss Prince had used. Potter had been trying to make a name for himself – his own name – since he started at Ranting Lane the term before. He climbed up on the photocopier, tugged his trousers and underpants down, pressed a button, and turned this way and that while the machine reproduced his backside from different angles. Most of the boys loved this. Most of the girls pulled faces. But then there was the sound of something breaking and everyone went quiet. Potter isn't a big kid, but even a smallish kid wriggling on the glass of a photocopier must have been weighty enough to break it, because that's what he'd done. He jumped off, hauled his togs up, grabbed the prints he'd made, and started back over the desks that were now jamming the aisles.

'Let's see, let's see!' cried Pitwell, snatching the photocopies as Potter climbed by.

Several others said the same thing, but before Pitwell could pass them round the door opened and Mr Hurley shimmied in. The big fat grin didn't last long this time, maybe because of all the yelling and people clambering over or standing on the desks. The shrill little voice of Julia Frame shouting, 'Stop it, stop it, take a card!' didn't help, specially when he saw the state of the photocopier. We denied everything, naturally, and just for once no one pointed fingers. We tried jollying him along with friendly stuff like, 'Bet you're looking forward to sending those passengers to sleep with History, eh, sir?' but we'd blown it. He was Surly Hurley again until the aisles had been cleared of desks, and there wasn't much lesson time left after that.

He didn't see the photocopies, though. Not till next morning anyway, when Pitwell and a couple of his mates hung them all round the main hall just in time for Assembly. Mother Hubbard was hopping mad when he saw them. He knew that the bum in the prints belonged to someone in our class because Hurley had told him that it was in his lesson that the copier got broken. He also knew it was a boy's behind, don't ask me how, I've never studied the difference. He kept the boys of our class *behind* (ho-ho!) and asked the culprit to step forward. No one moved. Potter was at the back, near me and Pete, almost wetting himself. I got the feeling that he didn't want to make his name any more. But he might as well have signed each print because on every left buttock in every one there was a wart like you'd expect to see on a hog, and he was the only boy in our class with a wart just there. (The teachers didn't know this, but you can't hide bum warts in the showers after Games, so even if we hadn't seen him butt the copier every boy would have known it was Potter's.) Gradually, all eyes found their way to him. They couldn't help it. It was like they were drawn to him by magnets. Hubbard finally got the message and looked directly at Harry (pretty red in the face by this time) as he said:

'For the last time before I suspend the lot of you for a very long time, who is responsible for this *childish* act?'

And Potter stepped forward. 'Me, sir,' he said in a trembly little voice.

'You did this?' Mother Hubbard said.

'Yes, sir.'

'Oh.'

It was obvious what that 'Oh' meant. It meant that Potter would get a detention and a note to his parents but nothing more major. If it had been me or Pete or Ryan or Atkins, or almost any other boy, we'd have been suspended from the school battlements if there were any, but not Harry Potter. If they'd suspended him, local radio might have picked it up, then TV, then the big national papers. The tabloids would have had a field day. Reporters would be hanging round the school gates for a week. Why? Why do you think? Because of the poor sap's *name*, of course!

Chapter Four

Like I said, most of the rest of that school day was pretty average. Average as in dull. There wasn't the teensiest hint that everything was going to go banana-shaped by home-time. I didn't pay attention to most of the day anyway. Other things than school on my mind. At lunch in the Concrete Garden, where the Musketeers have a private bench and swap crisps and sandwiches every weekday, Ange asked me what was up.

'What makes you think something's up?'

'Well, you're not your usual self today.'

'What's my usual self?'

'Oh, I don't know. Chirpy, sarcastic, critical…'

What I didn't tell her, or Pete, was that I was worried about my mum. Just a bit, you understand, nothing major. Did I mention that she threw up that morning and blamed it on last night's prawn curry? Who did she think she was kidding? Well I know who she *thought* she was kidding, but she'd hardly touched that curry so who did she think believed that was what had made her sick? Then I remembered that she hadn't been eating much of anything lately, and she wasn't looking so hot either. I also remembered the hospital appointment that she and my father didn't want to talk about in front of me. She was going there to have 'something checked', she said. What something? Dad was even taking the day off work to go with her, so it had to be serious. And what about last night's ironing lesson? Mum had never tried to show me how to iron before. And the reason she gave for showing me?

'If anything happened to me, you wouldn't know what to do.'

If anything happened to me. Like she thought it might – soon!

As the day trudged on, and me with it, I got more and more worried. We don't always see eye to eye, Mum and me, or even nose to nose. We have rows. We shout at one another. She tells me off for being sarky, or lazy, for not doing my homework or tidying my room, or making my bed like she asked, all sorts of stuff, and I make fun of her hair, her clothes, her suicidally depressing TV soaps. But she's my mum.

The only one I've got. I can't go to IKEA for a replacement. Mothers don't come in flat packs. They're flesh and blood and nail polish. They have to be there from the start, so they can be trained in the ways of the real world (slowly in my mother's case) by their super-smart kids.

The final lesson of the afternoon was RE. We had a newish teacher for this. Our previous RE teacher, Mr Prior, finally gave up after his third nervous breakdown and went off to do something less stressful than try and ram superstition into our disbelieving skulls.* His replacement – Mr Staples – was just as bald as Mr Prior, but he grew his hair extra long on one side and combed it over his dome to try and kid the world he was fully thatched. Mr Staples wore a dark-blue blazer with silver buttons, and he had holiday-camp-type badges all down both lapels, except they weren't holiday camp badges, they were badges for religions. I only knew one of them, the fishy one, because some people have it on the back of their cars alongside CLEAN ME. When we asked about the badges on his lapels during his first lesson, Mr Staples said, 'Each of these badges represents a different faith.'

---

* Rowing forwards across the Pacific, the rumour was.

So we got started. Well, you have to test the water with new teachers, don't you? See how far you can prod them before they burst.

'What's a faith, sir?'

'It's a religion. Surely you know that.'

'How many religions are there, sir?'

'Quite a lot.'

'Why so many, sir?'

'Oh, you know, different cultures...'

'Do you believe in all the religions you've got badges for, sir?'

'My personal beliefs have no bearing on this lesson, but no, I wouldn't go so far as to say that I believe in all of them.'

'So why are you wearing their badges?'

'Because this lesson is about comparative religion, not just one.'

'What's comparative religion, sir?'

'It's the study of many religions.'

'Why are we doing that, sir?'

'Because the curriculum says we must.'

'Why does it say that, sir?'

'Because it's been decided.'

'Who by, sir – God?'

'No, not by God, by the people who make such rulings.'

'Do you know these people, sir?'

'I don't know them personally, no.'

'But you're still doing what they tell you.'

'Yes, it's my job to do so. Now please stop asking questions and let's get started.'

'Do all these religions have different gods, sir?'

'Well, no, most of them have the same god, though some know him by a different name.'

'Why doesn't God stick to just one name, sir?'

'It's not God who decides which name he's known by, it's Man.'

'Is that the same man who tells you to talk about all your badges?'

'I mean Man in general.'

'You mean a man who's a general, sir?'

'No, I don't mean that at all, don't be silly.'

'What does God think about that, sir?'

'What does God think about what?'

'About people calling him different names.'

'I really can't say, I haven't asked him.'

'Why don't you send him an email?'

'I don't think God has an email address.'

'Oh, he must have. Everyone has an email address.'

'I don't, and I don't want one.' (Julia Frame.)

'If all these religions have the same god, sir, why are they different?'

'That's quite a complicated subject, which we'll get to another day.'

'Which day's that then?'

'I mean some future lesson.'

'Oh, goody. Give us something to really look forward to.'

That was our first session with Mr Staples. Two or three lessons later, the Thursday I'm rattling on about, I stuck my hand up because I needed to go for a tinkle. I hadn't gone at lunch-time, hadn't thought of it, probably because I was worried about my mum, but my legs had been in a knot for the past twenty minutes. Another five and there'd have been a puddle on the floor that I'd never live down.

'Very well, Joseph, but be as quick as you can.'

'Jiggy, sir.'

'I'm sorry?'

'Jiggy, not Joseph. You want a badge for that too?'

Teachers. Such hard work.

I scooted along the corridor to the Boys, spurted

my orangeade with a gasp, washed the McCue hands like my mother's always yelling at me to, and stepped into the corridor. I'd just started the return to the RE room when I heard a voice from the other side of an approaching corner – Mr Rice's, which you can't miss even with cotton wool in your ears. I didn't want to bump into him just then. He'd probably have a go at me for chortling when he jogged into the lamp post on the way to school. I needed to hide till he went by. But where? The lavs were too far behind me now and there were no other corners to dive round. The only door in view was the one attached to the caretaker's broom cupboard, so I ran to it, hoping it was unlocked and there was no one on the other side of it. I turned the handle. The door opened. I looked in. Dark, great, no one at home. I stepped in. Closed the door smartly but quietly behind me.

I couldn't see a thing in there, but I'd got a glimpse of the interior as I jumped in and had a mental snapshot of brooms, mops, sponges, polish, and industrial-sized cans of spray to massacre the flies we get in herds at Ranting Lane. There was also a bucket to trip over, but my mental snapshot hadn't included that, so I tripped over it. When I tripped – not quite as silently as I would have liked – Mr Rice, who'd just reached the other side of the door, stopped talking. My mouth turned to sawdust. Maybe the person he was chatting to was Mr Heathcliff, the miserable broom honcho who never had much to say, which meant the door could open any sec and I would be discovered and lugged out by the scruff of whatever.

I felt my way through the blackness behind me, very carefully so as to not to fall over anything else or make any more noise, and hid in a row of smelly old workcoats hanging at the back. If the door opened now they'd only see me if they looked down and saw my lower legs and feet.

And I heard it, the door opening, but it closed again almost at once. Relief. I was safe. I waited for Rice to start talking loudly again in the corridor, but he didn't. He must have moved on without saying anything else. But to be on the safe side I decided to give it half a minute and stayed where I was amidst the smelly old workcoats.

When the half minute was up I started forward, step by careful step, hands raised like paws in front of my eyes in case something sharp felt like skewering eyeballs in the dark. I was still walking when I sensed that I wasn't alone in there. I stopped, spine tingling. I couldn't see anyone, of course, and there hadn't been a sound, but...

'Hello?'

This was me, but as I said it I thought I heard a kind of echo of it, like someone else had said the same thing at the very same instant. I was so spooked by this that I didn't care what I crashed into or tripped over or whose arms I ran into in the corridor. I rushed forward, and as I did so...

...I felt someone rush by me!

'Eeeek.'

I know for *certain* that two voices said this. I charged through the dark, slapped the door, tore it open, and shot out into the deserted corridor, blinking like a maniac. From there I looked back to see who'd been in the broom cupboard with me. Apart from the brooms themselves, and the mops, the tripping bucket, the tins of polish, the cans of industrial fly spray, the dusters, boxes, jars of screws, the brown workcoats at the back, and all the other stuff that school caretakers seem to need, it was empty.

Chapter Five

I strolled back to my RE lesson. Felt I ought to, seeing as there was still a quarter of an hour to go before home-time. Reaching the classroom I noticed a plaque on the door that I couldn't remember seeing before.

SPIRITUAL TECHNOLOGY

Spiritual Technology? Was that what they called it now? Must have missed that. Still, same old prehistoric mumbo-jumbo, whatever name it travelled under. I opened the door.

'Ah, Juggy, good of you to take the trouble to return to us,' said a voice as I entered the classroom.

'Eh?' I said.

This seemed a pretty good question in the circs. Why? Five reasons.

1. It was Mr Hubbard who'd spoken to me. Hubbard the Head, not Mr Staples, who'd been hosting the lesson when I went to water the pony.

2. Mother Hubbard had known me for more years that I wanted to think about, and unless my ears had deceived me he'd got my name wrong.

3. Eejit Atkins was sitting in the seat next to mine at the back, where Pete Garrett belonged.

4. Pete was sitting next to Martin Skinner, down the front.

5. Pete was wearing glasses – which he doesn't!

It was all very weird, but I didn't want to get into some big fat dialogue about what had gone down in my absence, so I mooched to my desk at the back like nothing was out of order.

'Face front, everyone!' Mr Hubbard said sternly when every eye in every head watched me go. Most of them faced front, though a few couldn't seem to tear their orbs off me. 'You'll have to catch up, Juggy,' he said to me as I sat down.

'Do my best,' I said. 'And it's Jiggy.'

'Excuse me?'

'I'll write it on the board for you if you like, so you can practice saying it till it sinks in.'

He looked kind of puzzled, but went back to talking about whatever it was he'd been talking about while I was out. I turned to Atkins, who like I said was sitting next to me without my say-so.

'What are you doing in Garrett's seat?' I whispered.

'What?' he whispered back.

'I said what are you doing in Garrett's seat?'

'What do you mean?'

'I mean what are you doing in Garrett's seat?'

'I always sit here. Garrett sits with Skinner. What have you done to your ears?'

'My ears? What about them?'

'They're not sticking out.'

'I didn't know they were supposed to.'

'But they *always* stick out.'

'Have you two finished at the back there?' Mr Hubbard asked.

I looked in his direction. Noticed that the whole

class had turned to gawp at me again.

'Almost,' I said. 'Give us a minute, will you?'

'I'm just filling McCue in on what he's been missing,' Atkins lied.

'Well fill him in afterwards,' Hubbard said. 'Turn *round*, everyone!'

There was quite a lot of whispering as everyone turned round a second time. Mr Hubbard waited impatiently for the last whisper to die, then carried on from where he'd broken off.

'What happened to Mr Staples?' I asked Eejit behind my hand.

'Who?'

'The comb-over king. I know he's not very memorable, but you can't have forgotten him already.'

'Jug, did you take something while you were out?'

'Take something?'

'And please explain those *ears*.'

'What is this ear fixation?' I said, touching one of my perfectly normal lugs. 'And who are you to ask questions anyway, talking like that?'

'Like what?'

'Like an ordinary human being.'

'I'm talking the way I always talk,' he said.

'No, you're not.'

'I am.'

'Atkins, you are definitely not talking the way you— '

'You two!' Mr Hubbard shouted. 'One more word and it's detention.'

We buttoned the lips.

Mr H glanced at the clock on the wall. Still a bunch of ticks to go. Maybe he was struggling, I thought. Counting the minutes to the end of the lesson because RE wasn't his subject. Spiritual Technology, I mean. Staples must have been called away and Hubbard had had to stand in for him and was just waffling his way to the bell.

'As today's session is almost up,' he said, 'I think we'll have a quick Q-and-A to see what we've learned to date.'

And then he started asking this string of questions I wouldn't have believed any teacher could dream up, and the class – including Atkins, in his new voice – gave answers you wouldn't believe either. All the questions and answers were given in dead seriousness, like everyone actually believed what they were saying, which they couldn't possibly. The scene went like this, starting with Mr Hubbard's first question, which was:

'Who was Xenu?'

And the first answer: 'The ruler of the Galactic Confederacy.'

'When was this?'

'Seventy-five million years ago.'

'And the Galactic Confederacy was...?'

'A union of stellar systems.'

'How many stars and planets were contained within those stellar systems?'

'Twenty-six stars, seventy-six planets.'

'One of those planets was Earth. What was the name of Earth in Xenu's time?'

'Teegeeack.'

'Apart from being the omnipotent ruler of the GC, what is Xenu's primary claim to fame?'

'He paralysed billions of people and brought them to Teegeeack.'

'Why did he do that?'

'Because his corner of the galaxy was overpopulated, and he was a meany.'

'How did Xenu bring the people here?'

'In a fleet of spaceships.'

'Space *planes*, Gemma. The Founder has written that they resembled 1960s aeroplanes. What did Xenu do with the prisoners once they landed?'

'He positioned the planes round volcanoes and put bombs in them. In the volcanoes, not the planes.'

'Sir?'

'Yes, Martin?'

'If Xenu wanted to kill all the people why didn't he just throw them out on the way to Teegeeack?'

'Xenu's thinking on this has not been passed down to us,' Mr Hubbard said. 'Were there any survivors after the bombs went off? Bryan, how about you?'

Ryan looked up from the football mag he was reading under cover of his desk. 'How about me what?'

'Were there any survivors of Xenu's bombs?'

He shrugged. 'Dunno. Don't care.' (Ryan, the Voice of *Sanity*?)

'Anyone else?' Mr Hubbard asked.

There was, but I didn't see who, just saw a hand

in the air behind some heads. 'No one knows how many survived,' this person said.

'The figure is indeed unknown,' said the man 'but a considerable number did survive. The physical forms of the majority perished, of course, but not their souls. Who can tell me the proper name for those souls?'

'Thetans, sir!'

'Well done, Julia. What happened to the thetans?'

'I know! I know!'

This was Pete, wriggling in the seat next to Skinner with his hand in the air. Pete Garrett was speaking up in *class*? Pete Garrett had an answer to a question like *that*?

'Yes, Peter?'

'They were taken to huge cinemas in the Canary Isles and Hawaii and places.'

'That's right. Where they watched…?'

'3D films for twenty-six days.'

'*Thirty*-six!' Holly Gilder cried.

'Correct, Holly!' Mr Hubbard turned to her. 'Can you tell me what kind of material the thetans were subjected to during those thirty-six days?'

'Propaganda, sir. Phoney religious stuff.'

'Excellent! And what happened to the thetans once they'd absorbed all this false information?'

Pete jerked his hand up again. 'They were put into the bodies that'd survived the explosions!'

'And that means…what exactly?'

'That everyone walking the Earth today has thousands of souls loaded with total crap,' muttered Ryan.

'Everyone except True Believers like us,' Mr Hubbard said. 'Now, just one more before we— '

Too late. The bell went. Just in time too. One more question and answer like the ones I'd just heard and my head would have pinged off my neck and bounced out the window to be pecked to pieces by pigeons.

I was in a bit of a daze as I grabbed my school bag and dragged it towards the door. Something had happened here while I was admiring my reflection in the urinal and hiding in the broom cupboard. Something that didn't make any kind of sense.

'Are you all right, Juggy?' Mother Hubbard asked as I reeled by.

'Is anyone?' I said. 'And it's Jiggy. Jiggy, OK?'

Close up, I noticed that he wore a little badge. Just one badge, shaped like a volcano. Whatever loopy religion he'd been banging on about, it wasn't one of the ones on Mr Staples' lapels.

Chapter Six

Everyone else left the classroom like normal kids – pushing, shouting, laying life-threatening hexes on one another – but me, I left like I'd just stepped off the scariest roller-coaster at the fair. Atkins was waiting for me outside.

'What is *wrong* with you?' he said.

'Wrong with *me*!' I cried.

'What do you mean?'

'You. You're like a different person.'

'Jug,' said a voice. Angie's. She'd got tangled up with some of the others in the corridor, broken free, was coming towards us.

'Hang on,' I said, shoving a finger in each ear and looking at both tips. (No wax.) 'My name. What is it again?'

'Which one?' said Ange.

'Which one? How many have I got?'

'Well, you've got Jug, Juggy, McCue, and right now Wallybrain.'

'What's this Jug-Juggy stuff?' I said.

'And your ears,' said Angie. 'How did you do that?'

'Do *what*? They're just my *ears*.'

I barged through the doors to the playground, where the throng of kids were trying to trip one another up on the way to the school gates. I saw Pete a little way off. His shirt wasn't hanging out for a change and his tie was done up properly, also for a change, and he was still wearing those glasses. I went over to him.

'What's with the specs?'

He scowled at me. 'What?'

'The bottle-tops. Where'd you get 'em, Zappa's Joke shop?'

'What's wrong with them?'

'What's wrong with them, Garrett, is that you don't wear glasses.'

'I do. I've worn glasses for years.'

'No, you haven't.'

'I have, haven't I?' he said to Angie, who'd joined us with Atkins.

'Never noticed,' she answered.

'Obviously you haven't either till now,' he said

to me. 'Why the sudden interest?'

'Well, we're buds.'

'Buds? You and me? Since when?'

'Since the three of us were bumps in our mothers' dodgy dungarees from Help the Pregnant.'

'The three of us? Which three?'

'You, me and Ange, who else?'

He looked at Angie. She looked at him. They looked at me.

'What are you on about?' they said together.

Before I could answer, we were interrupted – by Skinner.

'Come on, PG. Tea round mine tonight, remember.'

Pete (*PG*?) glared at me one last time, then went off arm-in-arm with Skinner. Skinner, who he's always saying is the kind of creep he wouldn't even use as a boot-scraper. I was still trying to get over this when I felt a finger and thumb on my left ear. I jerked my head away.

'What are you *doing*?'

'Trying to find out how you did it,' said Angie.

'Did what?'

She peered behind the ear. 'There's nothing there,' she said in a voice of wonder.

I shook her off and headed for the gates, but couldn't get through in a hurry because of the eager escape committee still filling the gap. When I finally made it I found that Angie was right behind me. With Atkins.

'Don't you have some monkey chums to go home with?' I asked him as we walked away.

'Only you two,' he replied in his weird new human voice.

It wasn't only his voice that was human either. He wasn't walking the Atkins walk: hunched over, dragging his fists, lower lip a landing strip for bluebottles. How come?

And then it came to me. The truth. My heels carved a dent in the pavement.

'OK, who came up with all this?'

They skidded to a couple of other halts on either side of me.

'All what?'

'The unnatural behaviour, the ear references, the name game, Garrett pretending to be pals with Skinner, the loony class about aliens – how did you get Staples and Hubbard to go along with *that*?!'

They stared at me like I was a plughole salesman from Mars. The stares of people who weren't going to admit they were fooling around. That did it. I can take a joke as well as the next kid, and probably the kid next to him, but enough was enough. They could milk their stupid gag as much as they liked, but without me. I stormed off. Walked the rest of the way alone.

When I reached the estate, and my street, and finally my house I would have gone in the front door but I'd forgotten the key Mum and Dad presented me with in a special box when I got out of hospital after my thirteenth birthday.* Because I couldn't get in the front door, I nipped up the alley a few houses along and round the back of the row. Our back gate is always kept bolted, so I had to haul myself up and reach over the top to get in. I did this, but couldn't feel the bolt. I reached further down. There it was. Must have misjudged the position. I yanked the bolt, swung in on the gate, jumped off it to rebolt it behind me, walked round the L-shape of our garden fence and saw something that made me almost trip over my

---

* If you don't already know why I spent my thirteenth birthday in hospital you'll have to read a thing called *Ryan's Brain*. You need your frontal lobes examined if you think I'm going through all that again here.

toes. My kennel wasn't there. The kennel I'd made so lovingly in woodwork for the dog we didn't have, never wanted, had no plans to get. The fact that I'd made it for a non-existent dog didn't give anyone the right to chuck it. I'd have some strong words for the parental types when they got in from work.

Next stop, the garden gnome that stands beside the step. He was the next stop because the key to the back door is stored in the hole Dad drilled in his little red bottom. But…

No gnome. I glanced around. No sign of him. They'd dumped him too? When? Overnight, while I was asleep?

I looked around in case they'd only moved the gnome, but he wasn't anywhere. That left me with a problem. How could I get in the house if there was no garden gnome with a hole in its backside?

But then I noticed something else. Quite close to where our trusty old gnome has stood since Dad won it in a raffle stood a fairy. A stone fairy, with stone wings. So my parents had swapped our fat, scowling, hairy old gnome for a soppy, smirking, unhairy fairy. Well, I wouldn't miss him much, but

I hoped Dad had run a drill into the fairy's behind too. I got down and peered under her little stone skirt. No hole.

I got up and kicked the fairy. Tinkle. No, that wasn't its name, it was the sound of a key dropping from under one of its sickeningly cute little wings. I picked the key up and shoved it in the lock. I turned it. The door opened. I went in, miffed that no one had told me they'd dumped my beautiful kennel and traded in the gnome. For that I was going to empty the entire biscuit tin into my trap, and if my mother got uppity at tea-time because I didn't eat the lousy processed food she put in front of me, I'd let her have it. I would not be treated like this. Who did these parents think they *were*?

I slammed the door and lobbed my school bag into the corner where it spends most of its life. Thought the house smelt slightly unusual, but shrugged. My old lady's always experimenting with smells. I was halfway through the kitchen door when I skidded to a halt like a flying haddock had socked me in the kisser. The cupboards, the phoney quarry tiles, the aprons on a hook, none of them were the same as the ones I'd ignored at breakfast. Even the fridge magnets were different. Even the calendar. The calendar (Mum's choice) should have shown famous paintings I didn't know. This one didn't have famous unknown paintings. It had photos of muscle-men and muscle-women with sparkly grins. Dad might have chosen one like that – the muscle-women anyway – but if he'd tried to hang it Mum would have hung him there instead.

I just stared, stared and stared some more. Could they have had workmen in to totally remake the kitchen while I was at school? Was that even *possible*? I felt a worry coming on. My legs starting to twitch. Then my feet started to soft-shoe. Then my elbows started to flap. In twenty seconds I was jigging round the kitchen like a ballet dancer with ants in her knickers.

I forced myself to stand still. Wasn't easy, but I managed it. I rubbed my eyes, hoping I'd imagined all this. When I stopped rubbing, I looked again. No change. This was crazy. I knew my own house. Ought to, I'd been told off in it enough times, done enough rotten homework in it. But this didn't look like my house, even though the rooms and walls and doors were in the right place. Was it possible that I could have walked into the wrong one by mistake? I went out to the hall, opened the front door. The broken street lamp was still by the gate where it should be. It was my house all right. So what *was* this?

Because I couldn't make sense of any of this, I felt a sudden need to hide myself away while my brain unsteamed. I staired it up to my room, went in, shut the door, leant against it with my eyes closed. What an afternoon. First, Mother Hubbard talking seriously about aliens. Then Pete being friends with Skinner but not me. Now this. I took a bunch of long, slow breaths, eyes still closed, and started to feel better. Whenever the world does one of its back flips and a fresh batch of weirdness starts up, I always have my bedroom, my sanctuary. Nothing can touch me there. I opened my eyes, smiling, and...

That wasn't my wallpaper!

That wasn't my chest of drawers!

That wasn't my anything!

And where was my bed? There wasn't any kind of bed. Unless you counted the cot.

Yes, a cot. A baby's cot. I rushed to it. A little brown teddy-bear stared up at me, all glassy-eyed like it had been drinking.

I had never seen that teddy in my life!

I flung myself at the door, tore it open, and tottered downstairs like a Really Golden Oldie. I returned to the back door and whipped my mobile out of my bag. I don't usually take my phone to school because they don't like us using them in class for some reason, but I had that day, don't remember why. I punched digits. A voice answered.

'Ange,' I said. 'I think I've lost it.'

'Yes...' she said, like this wasn't something new.

'I'm at my house. Except that it's not.'

'I don't get you.'

'The house I lived in when I left this morning, number 23, seems to have other people living in it.'

'Number 23? Since when have you lived with Mr Rice and Miss Weeks?'

'Uh?'

'When you say you're there,' Angie said, 'you mean outside, right?'

'No, I mean in the back hall.'

There was a pause. Then she said, 'How'd you get in?'

'The stone fairy in the garden.'

'Mr Rice has a stone fairy?'

'I don't know what Mr Rice has. What I do know is there's a fairy where my gnome should be and everything in the house is different too.'

'Juggy,' said Angie.

'Jiggy,' I said.

'What's going on?' she said.

'You tell me,' I said. 'Ange. Do me a favour. Come over. This is turning into an all-for-lunch emergency.'

'A what?'

'Just get here. Please.'

She sighed heavily, but said, 'Oh, very well. Stay there. But outside. I'll be there in ten.'

'Ten? Ten minutes? Angie, this is a crisis. I need you now!'

'Yes, well it takes eight minutes walking fast to get to you from my side of the estate and I'm not working up a sweat for you when I know you're messing me about.'

'What do you mean, your side of the—?'

She clicked off before I could complete the question.

My cheeks puffed themselves out. My head shook itself. I'd never been great at maths, but suddenly nothing, I mean *nothing*, added up. I had a feeling that even two and two might have a struggle making it to four right now.

Chapter Seven

I needed something to lean against, so I spined the busted street lamp outside the front gate and gazed across the road to where Angie had lived almost as long as I'd lived at *The Dorks*. That very morning I'd seen her and Pete shove one another off the step before joining me in the street to drag our bags to school like we do every morning except Saturdays, Sundays, holidays, and anytime we can con our parents that we're not well enough to go.

I also knew where I lived, but suddenly my insane PE teacher, the Deputy Head and a glassy-eyed brown bear seemed to be living there instead. Not only that, but there was a stone fairy in the back garden and no dog kennel for the dog we didn't have. There were even different aprons and a different calendar in the kitchen. Crazy or what? Crazy or not, it wasn't until Angie finally dawdled along the street that my jaw hit my chest.

'What's with the fancy dress?' I gasped.

'She looked down at herself. 'It's just an ordinary dress.'

'Yeah, but it's pretty. It's all…girly.'

'I am a girl,' she said. 'I like pretty things.'

It was the first time Angie had ever said that, but I shook myself. More important things to talk about.

'Is Pete coming?'

'Pete?'

'Thought you'd have brought him. He likes to be in on these things.'

'Do you mean Pete Garrett?'

'What other Pete do you know?'

'I don't. Why would I bring Pete Garrett with me?'

'Because he lives with you?' I prompted.

'He what?'

'Because he lives with you.'

She scowled. 'Look, I've got things to do at home. If you're living out some fantasy here, let's get it over with, shall we – inside?'

'Inside?'

'Your skanky peasant house.'

'That's just it,' I said. 'I don't know which

79

is my skanky peasant house.'

'You were serious about that?'

I kicked the wall of number 23. 'This morning I lived here. Now I don't. Care to explain that?'

'Have you got your front door key?' she asked.

I ground my teeth patiently. 'If I had my front door key, why would I have gone round the back and looked up a fairy's skirt?'

'How would I know? Maybe it's your hobby. Come with me.'

'Where to?'

She didn't answer, so I followed her a couple of doors along, then down the alley I'd gone down earlier, then to the back gate of number 25, Mrs Overton's.

'Up you go,' she said.

'Up I go what?'

'The gate.'

'I can't do that.'

'Course you can. Used to do it all the time before you got the front door key you don't have today.'

'I went up *that* gate all the time,' I said, pointing to the next one along.

She sighed. 'Have it your way, but get up this one now.'

So I climbed the Overtons' gate. Climbed it, threw my arm over the top, found the bolt, no trouble, yanked it, swung in, jumped down.

'After you,' I said, standing aside because I'm such a gentleman. She was just walking through when I noticed something I'd missed before. 'Ange, how long's your hair been that colour?'

'What colour?'

'That reddish tint.'

'About a month.'

'I never noticed.'

'Why would you? You're a boy.'

She walked along the path. I closed the gate quietly behind me but didn't bolt it. I didn't feel right about this. We were trespassing on someone else's property. Suppose Mrs O or Dawn were in and saw us from a window? Would they call the cops? Would we end up in some cellar having lights shone in our eyes while men in braces threatened to tear our toenails out if we didn't talk?

The Overtons' house was just like ours – I'd been inside it a couple of times with Mum – but their back garden wasn't the same shape. You still had to go round a bit of fence to get to the house, though. I followed Angie round the bit of fence, and saw...

'My kennel!'

Yes, there it was, my woodwork project dog kennel.*

'Hey, some guard-dog you are,' Angie said.

'What do you mean some guard-dog I am?'

'Not you, toggle-brain – Stallone.'

'Stallone? My cat?'

'Your cat?'

'Yes, my cat, my cat.'

'Woof.'

That wasn't me. Wasn't Angie either. It was this big black beast that had just looked out at us.

'There's a dog in my kennel!' I cried, freezing to the spot.

Dogs do that to me, freeze me to spots. All dogs except china ones, plastic ones and the long hot ones you get in rolls with onions. Big black ones that flash their munchers as they lurch towards me are the worst. That's what the dog from my kennel was doing right now. When this enormous stunt double for the Hound of

---

* The kennel woodwork project happens in *Maggot Pie*.

the Baskerwillies reached me, it — well of course!
— sniffed my crotch.

'Get it off me!' I yelled, reaching for the clouds.

'He's not doing anything,' Angie said.

'He's sniffing my zip!'

'He always does that.'

'Now he's licking it!'

'That's because he loves you.'

'I never saw this monster in my life before! It's sure not Charlie Farnsbarns, and I don't like him either.'

'Charlie who?'

'Farnsbarns. Who lives here. In the house, not my kennel.'

Angie laughed. 'Here, Stallone, come to someone who likes you.'

The hound turned to her and licked her outstretched hand.

'Stallone?' I said.

'His name,' she said. 'Haven't we been over that?'

'But Stallone's a cat.'

'Quiet, you'll give him an identity crisis.'

'He's licking your hand,' I said.

'Yes. Sweet.'

'Sweet? How can you stand all that gloop running down your wrist? And that tongue could have been anywhere.'

'Not anywhere,' Angie said. 'It's been here with him in the garden all day.'

'It's been at my zip.'

'Apart from that.'

'Before that it was probably licking *his* zip.'

Her face twisted like an old rag and she pulled her hand away from the mutt's gleaming tongue. 'That's one image I did *not* need.'

She wiped her hand on my arm. I shuddered and took my jacket off. Held it by the loop in the collar as far away from me as I could get it.

Angie carried on along the path and I stepped carefully round the dog to follow her. The thing growled at me. Once they get the zip-love out of their system dogs always growl at me. They probably sense that I'm not a massive fan.

As I went after Angie I saw something familiar beside the back step.

'Our garden gnome!'

'Oh, something you recognise,' she said sarcastically.

When I reached the gnome I stooped, felt his bottom, found his hole, pulled the key out.

'Now what?'

'Now open the door,' said Angie.

'But it's not my door,' I protested.

She snatched the key, shoved it in the lock, turned it, flipped the handle, opened the door. When she handed the key back, I re-inserted it in the gnome's rear end and followed her inside, along the hall, into the kitchen. My feet locked just inside the doorway. I gaped around. It was my house's kitchen. My kitchen's cupboards and blinds and phoney quarry-tile floor. My mother's famous unknown paintings calendar was on the wall. Even the fridge magnets looked right.

'I...I...I...' I said, pronouncing all the vowels very carefully.

Angie leant against a cupboard and folded her arms, waiting to see if I could go on to construct a full sentence.

'Ange,' I said, taking a stab at it. 'I've lived next door to this house ever since we moved to the estate, but...'

'But?'

'I gotta check upstairs.'

I scampered up the stairs, too agitated to remove my shoes, like Mum insists whenever anyone goes upstairs. Angie followed more slowly.

On the landing, I pushed back the door of what would have been my room if this had been my house. Pushed it kind of timidly, no idea what to expect. I looked in. It was my room all right, but it was so much neater and tidier than my room knew how to be except after one of Mum's blitzes. And the bed. When I left it that morning, the pillows were in knots and the duvet was half on the floor. This bed was made. Perfectly made. How come? Mum wouldn't have had time to make it before going to work. *So who had made my bed?*

I was about to go in when I noticed that the third bedroom door on the landing was open. In my house, my actual house, that's the room we chuck all our junk in so no one can come to stay. I couldn't see any junk through the bit of open door, but I could see something else, something that shouldn't be there. I went to the door and pushed it back. No junk. Not one bit. But...

'Whose is that?' I said in amazement.

Angie joined me at the door. 'Whose is what?'

'That bed. Who's using this room?'

She didn't tell me. She said, 'Oh, this is getting too boring. You don't want my help, you want to just string me along some more. I have better ways of wasting my time than playing some stupid game with *you* boys.'

This annoyed me as much as she was pretending to be annoyed by me. I gave her a heavy scowl.

'I am not,' I said firmly, 'playing some stupid game.'

'Is that a fact?' she said, starting downstairs.

'Yes, it's a fact,' I replied, going after her.

She was halfway down when the front door bell rang. It rang again, for a bit longer, before she'd quite reached the bottom. Then the letterflap opened and a little kid's voice shouted through.

'Joseph! Joseph, I know you're in, I can see your bag down the hall! Let me in, I need a weeeeee!'

'Joseph?' I said. 'Is whoever that is calling me?'

'Who else calls you Joseph?' said Angie. 'Who else is *allowed* to?'

She opened the door. A little girl in a green school uniform rushed in from the step. 'Hi, Ange!'

the girl said, scampering past her and into the downstairs cloakroom.

'And I suppose you don't remember her,' Angie said.

I stared at the closed khazi door. 'Remember her? I never saw her in my life.'

'Better not try that one on her. She'll be most upset.'

'Why would she be upset?'

Angie glared at me. 'Because she's your little SISTER, Jug. Who thinks the sun shines out of your armpits!'

And she went, slamming the front door behind her.

Chapter Eight

I was kind of stuck for a minute. Couldn't move, couldn't think. There I am in the house next door, which all of a sudden seems to be my house, and we have a mangy dog called Stallone instead of a mangy cat called Stallone, and someone I don't know uses the junk room as a bedroom, and there's this little kid, this girl I'm supposed to believe is my sister, in the downstairs toilet that my mother calls the 'cloakroom', even though none of us hangs a cloak in there, or even has one. Some wild things had happened to me in my time, but whatever was happening here was shaping up to be the wildest yet. When I heard the toilet flush, my toes started to twitch. One more second and my feet would be dancing me up the wall. I had to give them something useful to do, so I ordered them to run me back up to the bedroom that looked like mine only tidier. I closed the door behind me, and, because there was no lock on it, jammed the chair under the handle to stop anyone coming in. With the chair in place my feet started to calm down. I sat on the bed. Safe!

But then...

Footsteps. Coming up the stairs. My spine shot me to attention.

'Joseph?'

The girl. Calling me. By the name no one gets away with.

Then she was knocking on the door.

I didn't answer.

She knocked again. Said 'Joseph' again.

I still didn't answer. I felt trapped. This small but total stranger was knocking and calling me by the forbidden name and there was nowhere to go except—

I looked at the window. All I had to do was open it and...

No. It would hurt.

The girl turned the handle, but the door stayed shut. To make extra sure it would hold, I jerked my lower portions off the bed and jammed my feet against the chair. I was now lying with the top half of my back on the bed and my legs stretched out like a bridge between it and the chair.

'Joseph, let me in!'

I said nothing. The door handle rattled.

'JOSEPH! STOP MESSING ABOUT!'

I continued to say nothing, but I was getting more nervous by the minute. It might only be a little kid on the other side of that door, but it was a little kid who was making out that she knew me and expected to be let in. I eyed the window again. If I whipped my foot off the chair, would I make it down to my mother's favourite rose bush before the kid pushed the door in? All right, I might break an arm or leg, but I still had another one of each. Of course, if I broke my neck I didn't have a spare, but maybe I—

'JOSEPH McCUE, I WON'T SPEAK TO YOU EVER AGAIN IF YOU DON'T OPEN THIS DOOR RIGHT *NOW*!'

This was followed by some kicks on the wood. I suddenly wished Angie hadn't shoved off. This wasn't a situation for one lone Musketeer, specially a male one. Be even better if Pete had been there too. Then I could have stood behind them, peering between them. But they weren't there, either of them. It was just me, under siege from this pint-sized brat who didn't sound like she was going to give up and leave quietly any time soon. There was no alternative. I had to face this. Face the little person on the other side of the door. Find out why she was in my house, pretending to be my sister, calling me by *that* name.

Heart all thumpety-thump, I took my feet off the chair and slid off the bed. I went to the door. She was still kicking it, still shouting to be let in. I took the chair away, but kept the toes of one foot against the door.

'Whaddayawant?'

'I want to come in and talk about school!' the kid said.

'Why?'

'Why? Because it's what we always do!'

'No, we don't.'

'We do. Always!'

'Who are you?' I asked through the door.

'What?' she said on the other side of it.

'I said who are you?'

'What do you mean who am I?'

'I mean who are you?'

'Who am I?'

'Yes! Who are you?'

There was a pause. Then she shouted again — 'Joseph McCue, let me iiiiiiiiiiiiiiiiiiiiiiiin!' — and kicked the door again. And again. And again.

Pint-sized or not, the kid was obviously a violent type. I couldn't take any chances with someone like that. I looked around for something to bash her with when I opened the door. The only thing that wasn't attached to something else and could be lifted was a table-tennis bat I keep for bouncing ping-pong balls up and down on when I'm really, really bored. But to get to the table-tennis bat I would have to take my foot off the door, and if I took my foot of the door the kid might choose that moment to try the handle again, and if she tried the handle again she'd be able to open the door and come in, which I didn't want her to do before I had a good grip on that bat. But I had to chance it. So I took my foot off the door and made a dash for the bat. And while I was dashing...

...the kid tried the handle. Opened the door. Came in.

I grabbed the bat. I whirled. I stood there, a lean,

muscular, terrifically macho fighting man, ready for anything, even terrifying small girls.

'Come any closer and I'll whack you!!!' I shrieked manfully.

And she…put her little fists on her little hips.

'What is wrong with you?' she demanded. 'What have I done?'

'How about trespassing, for starters?' I boomed heroically.

'Trespassing? In your room? You never minded before.'

'Before? I never laid eyes on you before!'

'Joseph,' she said, removing the terrifying fists from the terrifying hips, 'what is it? Are you in trouble at school? Tell me about it.'

'What?' I said.

'Tell me about it,' she repeated.

'You tell me,' I said.

'Tell you what?'

'What you're doing here and who you are. Also, while you're at it, why I'm suddenly living in the house next door.'

She pulled a puzzled face, but I wasn't fooled. This was a set-up, no doubt about it. She took a step towards me. I raised the table-tennis bat. One swipe would ping-pong her out the door. She reached up, closed her little hand round my muscular wrist like someone stupid enough to imagine they had the strength to stop a person as dynamic as me – and lowered my arm. Yes, she lowered my arm. Not with superhuman strength, not with any strength much, but just by doing it. When it came to it, I couldn't ping-pong her. Why not? Because of the way she was looking at me. Because of her big blue eyes and her little worried face, and her spiky all-over-the-place hair.

'Joseph,' she said, as gently as someone twice her height and four times her age, 'sit down and talk to me.'

I sat down on the bed. She sat down beside me. Took my hand. Held on to it. Listened while I said that I didn't know what was going on, didn't know why my bedroom and everything else was in this house instead of the one next door, or why my cat was a dog, or why there was a fairy in the garden instead of a gnome, or why Garrett was chums with Skinner instead of me, or why Eejit Atkins spoke like a human being, and that I didn't know her from a daughter of Eve.

'I see,' she said when it was all out.

'You do?' I said.

'No, but it's very interesting.'

'Interesting? It might be to you. To me it's plain crazy.'

'Yes, that too. You really don't know me?'

'I really don't. Who's behind this?'

'Behind it?'

'Well, it's obviously someone's warped idea of humour at my expense.'

'Do you really believe that?' the little girl said.

'I don't know what I believe.' I never said a truer six words.

She let go of my hand and rolled her sleeves up.

'What are you doing?' I asked, thinking that she was going to try and slap some sense into me or something.

'Just getting comfortable,' she said. 'We have some serious sorting out to do here. First, tell me about your ears.'

'Why does everyone keep asking about my ears?'

'Because they're not the ears we're used to seeing on that head. Mind if I look behind them?'

'What for?'

'May I?'

'Well…OK.'

I leaned my head down. She cleared the hair away and inspected the area behind my lugs. I was glad I'd washed back there only last month.

'Have you done something to them?' she asked.

'Like what?'

'Well, they're not right.'

'No, one's left, it's the way ears are.'

'I mean they're not the way my brother's ears should look.'

'Why should they? I'm not your brother.'

'But you look like him in all other ways.'

I shook her off my ears. 'I do?'

'You want me to show you?'

'I think you'd better.'

She got off the bed and went to the door. 'Don't go away.'

'Where would I go?' I said.

'And keep that door open!' she shouted as she ran downstairs.

I didn't move the whole time she was gone. Just

sat there, mind as empty as a footless shoe.

When she came back she was carrying a framed picture that she kept turned away so I couldn't see it.

'What's that?'

'A photo of my brother, who everyone except me calls Juggy.'

'Juggy,' I said. 'People keep calling me that. My name's Jiggy.'

'Jiggy?' she said. 'Funny name.'

'And Juggy isn't? Why does everyone except you call your brother Juggy?'

'I don't call him it because I think it's insulting. Even when I was little I wouldn't call him it. And Joseph's such a nice name.'

'Matter of opinion. Why is he Juggy to everyone else?'

She turned the picture she'd gone down for. I leaned forward to look at it. An enlarged holiday-type snap of her and her brother. Couldn't have been taken more than a year ago, because she didn't look much different. And her brother...

Was me.

Almost.

There was one thing about him that wasn't like me. The ears. My ears lie pretty flat, like the ears of most people who aren't royalty. The ears of the Jiggy in the photo didn't lie flat. They stuck out like they were held by invisible hands. They looked like jug-handles.

'Juggy...' I murmured, staring at those hefty lugs.

And then I murmured it again. 'Juggy...'

And then I said, 'Holy ear-holes.'

Chapter Nine

I couldn't get my head round it, but the thought that someone was pulling one or more of my legs was fading. This little girl didn't look like she knew how to pull legs. She was so serious about all this. So sincere. And those big eyes of hers!

'But if you're not Joseph,' she said, 'who are you?'

'I am Joseph,' I confessed. 'It's just that no one calls me it.'

'I would if you were my brother.'

'Yeah, well I'm not. I'm nobody's brother.'

'But you look just like him. *Exactly* like him apart from the ears.'

I chinned the photo. 'He's welcome to those.'

'I can see why you're not called Juggy,' she said. 'But why Jiggy?'

'Because I jig about sometimes.'

'Jig about?'

'It's something that kicks in when I get nervous.

Doesn't your brother jig?'

'No more than anyone else.'

'That must be it then. I got the jigginess, he got ears.'

'And you're here instead of him,' the girl said.

'Yes, I was kind of getting that too.'

'So where's my brother?'

I said I wished I knew. Then I asked her what her name was.

'Swoozie,' she said.

'Swoozie?'

'My parents named me Suzie, but when I started to talk it came out as Swoozie, and that's who I've been ever since.'

I had a blood-freezing thought.

'If I'm not who I'm supposed to be, it must mean that no one's who I thought they were either. Now I know why Mr Hubbard was hosting the mumbo-jumbo class. And that that wasn't the Pete Garrett I know. Or my Eejit Atkins. Or Angie. And you, you're really who you say you are.'

'Of course I am,' said Swoozie McCue.

'But…how did it happen?'

'Good question. Another good one is where's my Joseph?'

'Maybe he's still here,' I said. 'Maybe he's on his way home from school and is just a bit late.'

'You think?'

'No, not really. He wasn't around when I left school with Atkins and Angie. Which means that right now, this minute, he's in my house, where he doesn't have a sister or a dog.'

Swoozie's eyes welled up with water. Her face crumpled.

'But that's terrible! Poor Joseph! He'll be so confused!'

'He's not the only one.'

'And lonely.'

'He'll get used to that. You do when you're an only child.'

'But he hasn't been an only child for years! There's no one to look after him if I'm not there.'

'Well, there'll be my mum and d...' I stopped. 'Woh! It's your mum and dad who live here, not mine.'

'I certainly hope so,' she said.

Then she plonked herself on the bed beside me.

The worried look was gone. She was all excited now, keen to get a handle on the situation. That's girls for you. They get used to stuff with a snap of a finger and thumb. Must be a gene thing. The get-over-it gene that only females have.

'What we've got to do,' she said, 'is try and work out how to switch you and Joseph back before anyone catches on.'

'Yes,' I said. 'Absolutely.'

'Looks like a job for the Three Cavaleiros.'

'The what?'

'The Three Cavaleiros. Joseph's gang. Don't you have Three Cavaleiros where you're from?'

'No. I've got Three Musketeers. Who are they, these Cavaloorolls?'

'Leiros. Joseph, Angie and Eejit.'

'Eejit? Eejit Atkins is a member of your brother's gang?'

'Of course. He's his best friend. Him and Ange.'

'Atkins is a moron,' I said. 'No McCue would be best friends with him.'

'Eejit isn't a moron. He's very bright. Joseph says he has to practically gag him in class to stop him answering every question.'

I thought about this. The Eejit I'd talked to earlier certainly hadn't seemed dumb. He was like a different species of Eejit. An Eejit that had survived evolution. Atkins Erecticus.

'So why do they call him Eejit?' I asked. 'I know why we call our Eejit 'Eejit' – he's as thick as a breeze block – but why would you call a bright person Eejit?'

'It's a joke,' said Swoozie McCue, the sister I didn't have.

'And he doesn't mind?'

'Doesn't seem to. Shall I phone them?'

I wasn't sure about that. They weren't my Angie and Eejit, and this place's Angie hadn't been very happy with me when she left and might not want to come back. I told Swoozie this. She grinned.

'I'll talk her round. You three need to put your heads together.'

'Seems like you're doing the job of three heads yourself,' I said.

She flashed me a big, pleased smile. 'Thanks, Joseph!' Then she remembered that I wasn't her brother. 'Is it all right to call you that?'

'I prefer Jiggy.'

'Doesn't sound right. And I can't call you Juggy, because people would wonder why I was doing it when I never do.'

'OK. Joseph. Just you.'

She beamed again. 'That's what my brother says. Just me.'

She started for the door. 'Where are you going?' I asked.

'To call Angie. My mobile's in my room.'

She didn't come back with her phone, but I heard her speaking in the room I was used to seeing junk in next door. When she returned, she said, 'Angie says she'll be round later if she's stopped crying, and she'll collect Eejit on the way.'

'Why's she crying?'

'She's chopping onions for tea because her dad's working late.'

'Her dad?'

'Yes, her dad. Why did your eyebrows just shoot up?'

'My eyebrows just shot up because where I'm from Angie's mum and dad split up aeons ago. Her mum's been living with Pete Garrett's dad since we were ten.'

'Pete Garrett's dad? Mr Garrett the boozer?'

'Boozer? Ollie likes his beer, but I wouldn't call him a *boozer*.'

'Well this one would live in a pub if they didn't keep chucking him out for being drunk and disorderly,' Swoozie said.

Suddenly I heard the front door slam. My body twitched, head to toe.

'Anyone at home?' a voice called from downstairs.

My mother's voice!

Swoozie went to the door and leant out. 'We're in Joseph's room.'

'All right. Just so I know.'

'I can't deal with this,' I whispered as she pushed the door to.

'You'll have to,' she said.

'How? She'll know I'm not her son. We'll have to tell her everything.'

She shook her head. 'She's a Golden Oldie. Think of all the kid-hours we could waste not being believed.'

She was right. Try and tell the GOs some slightly unusual fact and you might as well go back to bed and stuff your face in a pillow.

'She's bound to notice the ears,' I pointed out.

'Mmm, yes,' Swoozie said. 'The ears are a bit of a giveaway.'

'Bet he wishes he could,' I said.

'Bet who wishes he could what?'

'Your brother. Give his ears away.'

'He's used to them. We all are. When he was little, Mum taped them back, but the kids in the Infants made fun of him and he kept coming home in tears, so she had to stop. I wasn't born then, of course. I heard about it later. There was one boy in particular who really got on his case about the ear tape. Bryan Ryan. They've been arch-enemies ever since.'

'Good to know some things don't change,' I said.

'Oh, I know what we can do!'

She fell to her knees and felt under the bed. When she found what she was after she gave it a tug and came up with a ball of fluff-covered chewing-gum the size of a large plum. I had one under my bed just like it. I add more gum to it all the time. I have an ambition to get it as big as a grapefruit and eBay it to the highest bidder.

'Put it in your mouth,' Swoozie said.

I reared back. 'No chance. It's not mine.'

'Oh, you Josephs!' she said, and jammed it in her own little mouth. It was such a big gumball that it made her cheeks bulge. Can't have been easy to move it around but she did her best, and after a while forced it out again. Then she squeezed the gum with one hand while she picked fluff off her tongue with the other. The gum wasn't as solid any more.

I eyed it suspiciously. 'What are you going to do with it?'

She broke two bits off the gumball and pinched them to make them even softer. 'Turn round,' she said.

I turned round and, in no time at all, my faithful lugs were so much like sticky-out handles that my name could have been *Juggy* McCue.

chapter Ten

Let me tell you, that was one strange tea-time. I sat across from my borrowed sister, with my borrowed father at one end of the table and my borrowed mother at the other. The mother and father were like mine in almost every way. *Almost* every way. This mother's hair was a bit shorter than my mum's, and it had a green streak in it, and the father wore a little gold ring in his right ear. The hair I could cope with, but I couldn't help staring at the earring. Yeah, I know, a lot of men wear earrings, but the Melvin McCue I know would never have a hole drilled in his lobe and stick a ring through it.

And the way they spoke to me. My parents have this completely false idea that I'm going to do something childish or stupid every minute of the day and they're always on guard for when it happens so they can tell me off or ground me or deprive me of something till I apologise. But those two, they talked to me like I was a human being instead of a thirteen-year-old boy. I wasn't used to that, but to tell you the truth I kind of liked it. I still had to watch my mouth in case I put my feet in it, but Swoozie was always there to cover my tracks when I said something that seemed a bit odd to them. The thing is, this was a McCue family of four and I was used to a McCue family of three. Families of four have done things that families of three haven't, and it stands to reason that when there's an extra kid, and the extra kid's a girl, some of the things they've done are with her, and I wouldn't know about those things. A good example of something they did with her occurred that evening. Her mum was taking Swoozie for a ballet lesson. My mum never took me to ballet lessons. Normally, Swoozie went to ballet right after school, she told me, but the lessons had become so popular that some of the older students (which included her even though she was only eight) had been asked to take the later one. She didn't mind because it meant she could have her tea first.

The other Angie Mint arrived just after half-six. She'd phoned Eejit on the way and met him outside. This Eejit lived in the same house as my Eejit, only where I come from it's just over the fence, not next-door-but-one. When the dad-who-wasn't-mine let them in, they kicked their shoes off like people have to in my real home, and trotted upstairs. Swoozie only had a few minutes before she went to ballet, but she filled them in on the basics. When they didn't believe her right off she stood in front of them with her little hands on her little hips, and said, 'It's true! He's not Juggy, he's *Jiggy*!'

'What sort of name is Jiggy?' said Atkins.

I pulled a face at him. 'What sort of name's Juggy? Better still, what sort of name's Eejit? You have to be a prize-winning cretin to let people call you Eejit if you're not one.'

'He has a point,' Angie said to him.

Atkins grinned. 'Yeah, guess he has.'

To make sure they got it that I wasn't her brother, Swoozie showed them the chewing gum she'd wedged behind my ears. She even took one piece out so they could see how flat the ear went without a prop, and waggled it back and forth to prove that it wouldn't stay out when she let go.

After that they had to believe. When Swoozie left, they threw question after question at me. I won't bore you with them all because they were mostly the same ones Swoozie had asked after I let her into the bedroom, but there were two I couldn't answer.

1. 'How?'

2. 'When?'

'I'm guessing that the "when" was during Spiritual Technology,' the other Eejit Atkins said.

'Why then?' the other Angie asked.

'Because he was his usual self when he headed for the bogatorium, but when he returned his ears were flat and he wondered why I was sitting in Garrett's seat.' He looked at me. 'Wherever you're from, I can't believe you're friends with that bonehead.'

'Can't believe it myself sometimes,' I said. 'But it's Atkins who's the real bonehead there. How long have you and Juggy hung out together?'

'Couple of years. Since we realised we were better than anyone else at EI.'

'EI?'

'Then we started practising together, thinking up ideas, working out strategies, and here we are today, representing the school.'

'Representing the school in what?'

'Look, can we leave the background info till we've sorted out what happened here?' Angie said. 'We need to find out where Juggy went and how come his clone took his place.'

This got me. 'Hey,' I said. 'Get this straight. I'm nobody's clone. I'm a total original. A one-off. There is no other Jiggy McCue.'

'Maybe not,' she said, 'but there's a Juggy McCue, and only two obvious differences, both of them on the side of your head. You want to push that one out, by the way? Looks kind of weird, one ear like a wing, the other like a flapjack.'

My ears were that way because Swoozie had forgotten to rejam the gum behind the one she'd waggled for them. I replaced it and wiped my hand because it had been in two other mouths.*

'What's your pal like?' I asked when Ear Two was back in handle mode.

'Juggy?' Angie said. 'Except for the ears he's exactly like you.'

'No, I mean as a person. Is he loaded with character, charisma, charm, stuff like that?'

---

* The gum, not my hand

'Not that I've noticed.'

'But he's very witty, yes? Good with the one-liners, the rapid come-backs?'

'Not especially, no.'

I was shocked. This Juggy person was like me but he didn't have these essential McCue characteristics? But there was one thing my almost-double had to share with me.

'Tell me some of the insane things that have happened to him.'

The other Eejit Atkins and the other Angie Mint looked at one another like I was suddenly talking backwards in Swedish.

'Insane things? Like what?'

'Well, like…'

I took a long sorrowful breath, then ticked off the list, one tragic event after another.

'Like being haunted by a dead goose.' [1]

'Like his mother buying him underpants that take over his life.' [2]

'Like switching bodies with a girl and having to wear green knickers in netball practice.' [3]

'Like peeing a thousand and one times and conjuring up a teenage genie with dreadlocks

---

[1] *The Poltergoose*

[2] *The Killer Underpants*

[3] *The Toilet of Doom*

who makes him eat maggots.' [4]

'Like discovering a small green creature on the council tip that lives on human nose-juice.' [5]

'Like having all his clothes disappear in public places whenever he writes with a certain pen.' [6]

'Like sprouting a tail after being blackmailed by a puppet in a red bowler hat.' [7]

'Like wading through the slime in a giant slug's gut because he stepped aside in football practice.' [8]

'Are you talking about your nightmares?' Atkins asked when I'd finished.

'Wish I was,' I said. 'They're things that have happened to me.'

'You're not serious.'

'Wish I wasn't. Please tell me I'm not alone in the universe. Tell me that stuff like that also happens to Juggy.'

'If it does, he's been keeping it to himself,' said Angie.

Amazing. 'So there's absolutely nothing that makes your version of me stand out from the crowd apart from the ears.'

'Well, he's got us.'

'You?'

---

[4] *Maggot Pie*
[5] *The Snottle*
[6] *Nudie Dudie*
[7] *Neville the Devil*
[8] *Ryan's Brain*

'We're a sort of gang. Juggy, Eejit and me.'

'Oh yeah, I forgot. The Three Camelearoles.'

'Cavaleiros,' said Atkins.

'I've got a gang too.' I managed a smile. 'You could say I have a doppelgang.'

'Why would we say that?'

'Well, "doppelganger" is German for someone's double, and you have a gang and I have a gang, and…'

I fizzled out. They were looking at me strangely. I knew those looks. I get them quite often when I say terrifically intelligent things. People can't keep up.

'What's yours called?' Angie asked at the end of the silence that followed.

'My what?'

'Your gang.'

'The Three Musketeers.'

'The Three Musketeers? How boring.'

'Boring?'

'So obvious. So predictable. I bet that all over the world, whenever three kids want to form a gang, the first name they think of is the Three Musketeers. Except us. What's your motto?'

'We don't have a motto, we have a battle cry.'

'Oh, you go into battle, do you?' said Atkins with a smirk.

'Well, no, not exactly. We just sort of band together in times of stress and face the world shoulder to shoulder, toe to toe and back to back.'

'Contortionists then, are you?'

I glared at him.

'What's this battle cry?' Angie asked.

'You wouldn't be interested,' I said. I was quite miffed about the Musketeers being trashed like this.

'Why wouldn't we be interested?'

'Because you think the Three Commodes is a better name than the Three Musketeers.'

'Cavaleiros,' said Atkins.

'We don't think it's *better*,' Angie said. 'The Three Musketeers isn't a bad name, just an over-used one. Tell us your battle cry.'

I looked from one of them to the other. They seemed like they really wanted to hear our battle cry.

'All right.' I took a deep breath, puffed my chest out, and uttered it, slowly, in my deepest, most heroic voice. 'One for all and all for lunch!'

'What?' said Angie.

I repeated it for the hard of hearing. 'One for all and all for lunch!'

'One more time,' said Atkins.

'One for all and all for lunch.'

'That's your battle cry?'

'Yes.'

They fell to the carpet, chortling merrily. 'One for all and all for lunch!' they gasped. 'One for all and all for lunch! One for all and all for lunch!'

I scowled down at them. 'OK, so what's your brilliant battle cry?'

'Motto,' said Angie, staggering to her feet and deactivating the chortle.

'What's the Three Catatonics' motto then?'

'Cavaleiros,' said Atkins. 'And it's kind of a secret.'

'I promise not to tell anyone,' I assured him, thinking that maybe I'd spray-paint it on every wall in sight, first chance I got.

They looked at one another like two people who weren't sure they wanted to share their secret motto with a stranger who looked exactly like their best boring friend except for the ears.

But then they said:

'Well…all right…'

They crossed very serious arms over their chests so that each of their left hands rested on each of their right shoulders and each of their right hands rested on each of their left shoulders.

'The Three Cavalieros' secret motto is…' Angie said, and looked one more time at Atkins. He nodded, and together they spake their big deal motto.

'Hola! Hola! Hola!'

I waited for a minute for the dust to settle, then cleared my throat.

'Would you mind saying it again?'

They said it again.

'Hola! Hola! Hola!'

'Hola! Hola! Hola!?' I said.

'Yes.'

'You know what hola, hola, hola means?'

Angie removed her hands from her shoulders. 'Hello, hello, hello.' She looked kind of embarrassed, I thought.

'What are you, secret policemen?' I asked.

'We were young when we came up with it,' said

119

Atkins, shoving his hands in his pockets and drawing a circle on the carpet with his toe.

'Here's a thought,' I said. They looked at me expectantly. 'What do you say we don't mention your motto or my battle cry ever again as long as we live? At least while we're all in the same room together.'

They agreed.

'Maybe we could be a new gang with a new motto or battle cry while we figure out how to switch Juggy and Jiggy back,' Eejit said.

We agreed on this too and sat down on the floor, where we spent the next hour failing to decide on a new gang name. In the end, in desperation, we just called ourselves The Three. And our battle-cry-motto?

'Bam-kerchow!'

It takes a bunch of real geniuses to think up something like that.

Chapter Eleven

'Let's go back to Spiritual Technology,' the other Eejit Atkins said when the name of our gang was settled.

'Back to school?' said the other Angie Mint.

'I mean to what happened between the time Juggy left ST and Jiggy came back.'

'It's RE where I come from,' I said.

'What is?'

'ST. Was last time I checked the door anyway.'

'What does RE stand for?'

'Religious Entertainment. Your ST beats anything Mr Staples bangs on about though. Do you believe all that stuff that went down in class today?'

'That the human race was brought to Earth by an alien dictator and stacked around volcanoes while he blew them up and that the souls of the dead went to the pictures afterwards?' Angie said. 'What do you think?'

'You were pretty convincing.'

'It's a quiet-life thing. If we don't act willing, or give too many wrong answers, Hubbard says the Spirit of Xenu is in us or gives us detention where we have to read about all that twaddle, silently.'

'Ryan didn't seem bothered about that.'

'Yeah, well that's Ryan.'

'And Pete Garrett seemed genuinely interested.'

'Garrett and his pal Skinner are among the converts. They wear the badge, attend the voluntary after-school "spiritual expansion" chats, and cross their backsides every time they say the name Xenu. They're as crazy as Ronnie Hubbard himself.'

'We were talking about what happened today,' said Atkins impatiently.

It was still hard to look at him the way he was and get used to proper words coming out of his mouth. Eejit Atkins talking sense and behaving like something that didn't scratch its armpits in trees? What an unbelievable world this was. World. Yes. It was a different world all right, no doubt about it, and I had no idea how I'd got to it. Or had I...?

'Mr Heathcliff's broom cupboard!' I said suddenly.

'What about it?' Angie asked.

'Before I went in there everything was normal. When I came out it was like this.'

'This is normal.'

'Not to me it isn't.'

'What were you doing in Heathcliff's broom cupboard?' Atkins said.

'Hiding from Mr Rice. Hey, you haven't got a Mr Rice too, have you?'

'Sure we have. He's the Power Jogging and EI coach.'

I clutched my head. There was even a bozo in red here? Angie asked why I was hiding from Mr Rice. I declutched the head.

'He's always got it in for me because I'm not a sports nut. I try and keep out of his way. When I heard him coming, Heathcliff's broom cupboard was the nearest thing with a door to put between us.'

'What happened in there?' Eejit asked.

'I don't know if anything happened in there, but...'

'But what?'

'But now that I think of it…'

'Yes? What? Stop breaking off in the middle of sentences.'

'It was too dark to see, but I had a feeling I wasn't alone.'

'You think Heathcliff was in there too?'

'No, not Heathcliff. If he'd been in there the light would've been on. Besides, it didn't feel like him.'

'How could you tell if it felt like him if he wasn't there?' Eejit asked.

'I mean I sensed him. Not Heathcliff, someone else.'

But then it came to me. I stared at them both.

'You said your mate Juggy left your alien religion lesson, didn't you?'

'Yes.'

'Well, who's to say that while he was out he didn't pop into your Mr Heathcliff's broom cupboard when I popped into mine?'

'Why would he do that?'

'Same reason I did, to hide from a teacher. Yes, that must be it. We switched places, schools, homes, mates, the whole bunch of wahooley, because we're alternative versions of the same person who happened to go into Heathcliff's broom cupboard during the same pee break.'

'And you think the two of you passed in the dark and stepped out of one another's school broom cupboard,' Angie said.

'Exactly!'

Eejit stroked his beardless chin. 'That could be it,' he murmured.

'It *has* to be,' I said. 'And right now, this minute, your eary chum could be sitting in my bedroom with the remaining two Musketeers trying to work out the same things we're trying to work out here.'

'But things like that don't happen in real life!' Angie exclaimed.

I looked at her sadly. Enviously. 'Not in your life maybe.'

When Swoozie came home from ballet she rushed straight upstairs and threw back the door. 'What have I missed?' she demanded, standing there in her cute little pink ballet outfit.

We told her where we'd got to and she rolled her bright blue eyes in amazement. But then she came over all troubled.

'So right now my Joseph's in another room like this?' she said, looking around as if expecting to see him sitting in a corner or somewhere.

'Could be,' I answered. 'But next door.'

'I hope he's all right there.'

'He'll probably be as all right there as I am here.'

'Oh!' she said.

'What?' I said.

'School.'

'What about it?'

'He'll have to go to yours tomorrow.'

'Yes, and I'll have to go back to an alternative Ranting Lane.'

'Ranting Lane?' said Angie and Eejit together.

'Isn't that the name of your school?' I asked.

'No, ours is called Arnold Snit Compulsory,' Angie said.

'Arnold Snit? As in Councillor Snit?' She nodded. 'He's done well here then,' I said. 'He only got a park and a cul-de-sac named after him where I come from.'

'Lucky you. Here, half the town's got his moniker on it. There's Arnold Snit Parkway,

Arnie Snit Boulevard, the A.F. Snit Theatre of Contemporary Issues, The Snit Centre for Cheap Immigrant Labour, and Xenu knows what else.'

'He's popular then.'

'No, he's just good at blackmail. My dad says old Snitty's got every influential person in town in his pocket.'

Swoozie wasn't listening to any of this. She was still thinking about her brother. Worrying about him. Must be nice having a little sister who cares that much about you, I thought. When she heard that we'd formed a new gang to deal with the problem of me being there instead of her brother, she wanted to join us.

'You can't,' Angie told her. 'We're called The Three. You can't have four people in a gang called The Three.'

'We could change the name,' I said.

'We are not,' she said, 'sitting on this floor for a further hour to work out another name for our gang!'

'No need. We just call ourselves The Four.'

'The Four...' she said, chewing this over. 'Do you think it works without "Fantastic" or

"Famous" in the middle?'

'It works fine. And it's only for a while after all.'

'We don't know how long it'll be,' Eejit said. 'You might be stuck here forever.'

'Don't say that!' cried Swoozie. 'I want my brother back!' Then she realised what she'd said and turned to me. 'Sorry. I don't mean I want to get rid of you. If I could, I'd keep you as well.'

'It's OK,' I said. 'I want to get back to my family too.' And I'd never said *that* before. 'Look,' I said to the other two of The Four. 'If I got here via my school caretaker's broom cupboard, doesn't it stand to reason that to get back I have to go through the broom cupboard in your school?'

'Ye-es...' they said, though they didn't sound too sure.

'So that's what I'm doing at morning break tomorrow. I'm going into your Mr Heathcliff's broom cupboard and I'm walking out of my Mr Heathcliff's broom cupboard. Then all this will be behind us and we can get back to normal. Well, you can. Normal isn't in my vocabulary, except as a word.' I sighed. 'It's not fair, y'know.'

'What isn't?' the other Angie Mint asked.

'Some kids get nice old wardrobes, fur coats, snowy woods, fauns. But me, Jiggy McCue? Oh no. I get a caretaker's broom cupboard, stinky old workcoats, cans of fly-spray, and another school with Mr Rice!'

Chapter Twelve

It was a long night. A very long night. A night so long that I started to think that daytime had been cancelled. I did an awful lot of turning and tossing and sitting up in bed saying, 'Whaaaat?' but I must have slept eventually because I woke from something in the morning. And when I woke I realised that it had all been a dream. One bleary-eyed glance around was proof of that. Still, because it had been such a vivid dream I slid out of bed and looked for something extra to prove that I wasn't just in a very similar room. When I spotted my little Musketeer Rule Book on the desk I chuckled quietly with relief. I picked the book up fondly. On the cover, where I'd written our heroic battle cry 'One for all and all for lunch', were the immortal words…

'Hola! Hola! Hola!'

My knees sagged so fast I almost broke my jaw on the way down. I gripped the desk to steady myself. My feet started moving. My arms flapped. I would have yelled for Mum, but it wasn't my mum snoring in the room along the landing. Not my dad either. I was in the house next door to the one that would have been mine if I hadn't been here. This was probably the very room where Dawn Overton put on her bra in my world. I felt my eyes brighten. But then I felt them go dull again. Less interesting but more important things to think about. In this world Angie Mint lived in one of the rich people's houses on the other side of the estate, I was best friends with Eejit Atkins, and I had a little sister. Sister. Weird to think that I had a sister, even a borrowed one. But here's a funny thing. When I thought of Swoozie I calmed down right away. Stopped fox-trotting and flapping round the room. She was the only McCue in the house apart from me who knew I didn't belong there. I needed someone like that. Needed to speak to her. I crept to the door in the pyjamas I'd got out of the drawer the night before – even if the boy who slept in that bed was another me, I wasn't wearing his unwashed PJs – and went out to the landing.

The resident Golden Oldies' bedroom door was still closed, but Swoozie's was open just a bit. I tiptoed to her room and looked in. She was fast asleep.* She didn't actually have her thumb in her mouth, but it sort of sat there on her pillow, a few inches away like it really wanted to go in. I was thinking how sweet she looked lying there when she opened her eyes. Maybe she sensed me or something. She blinked the sleep out of her eyes and smiled.

'Hi, Joseph.'

'No, it's me,' I said. 'Jiggy.'

'I know.' She sat up. 'But still Joseph.'

'Can I come in?'

'Course.'

She patted her duvet. I sat down on it.

'Thought I might have dreamed everything,' I said.

'Well, you didn't,' she said.

'No. And…' My shoulders slumped. I went all feeble and helpless. 'And I don't know what to do about it.'

'Yes you do,' she said.

'I do?'

---

* Can anyone tell me why you have to be *fast* asleep? What's fast about sleep? The sleep I'd just come out of had been about as fast as a snail crossing Antarctica on crutches.

'Yes. You said it yourself last night. You're going to school and you're going into the caretaker's broom cupboard, and when you walk out you'll be back where you belong.'

'I don't know if it'll work.'

'No, but you have to try it.'

'If it does work, it won't automatically bring your brother back.'

'Maybe not, but when you get there you'll have to find him and tell him to do what you did, only the other way round.'

My knees puckered. 'You mean I have to talk to him?'

'Well, you could try signing, but talking might get the idea across more quickly.'

'It'll be like talking to myself,' I said. 'So… weird.'

'It probably will, but it has to be done.'

She was right. It had to be done.

'Morning!'

We turned to the door. Her mum was looking in.

'One of your early-morning chats?' she said.

'Joseph had a bad dream,' Swoozie told her.

'Oh, no.' She gave me a small concerned frown.

'You over it now?'

'Getting there,' I said.

But then: 'Juggy!'

'What?'

'Your ears!'

'What about them?'

'Well, they're… flat?'

The 'flat' came as a question, like she couldn't believe she was saying it. I felt my ears. I'd forgotten to put the gum behind them. How could I get out of this? But I needn't have worried. Swoozie was there.

'He must have been lying on them,' she said.

'You think that's it?' her mother said.

'Of course. They're often flat first thing. Haven't you noticed?'

'No, can't say I have. Fancy that. Now don't spend all morning chatting!' she said as she left us.

I turned gratefully to Swoozie. I obviously needed someone like her to watch my back. And my ears.

'Go on,' she said. 'Shoo. Big morning ahead of you.'

I went back to the bedroom that wasn't quite mine and mouthed the earballs to soften them. I stuck them where they had to be and fluffed out some hair to cover them. As I checked myself in the mirror to make sure I'd got the ear angles right I got to wondering how it would have been for Juggy if he'd done what I reckoned he had: stepped into my school when I stepped into his. From the broom cupboard he would have gone to the class he thought was his, and been puzzled to find Mr Staples chuntering about a bunch of fruit and nut religions instead of Mr Hubbard chuntering about just one. He would have been surprised to find Pete Garrett sitting next to him, and to hear that they were best friends. And what about Atkins? The Eejit Atkins of Ranting Lane was quite a different kettle of crabs to the one at A.S. Compulsory. Then, when school was out, this other McCue would have gone round the back of Janet and Dawn Overton's and not found a fairy with a key up her backside, and eventually realised that he lived next door, in the house he expected Mr Rice and Miss Weeks and their glassy-eyed teddy-bear to be living in. Finally, he would learn that Angie Mint didn't live on the rich side of the estate but just across the road, with Garrett and his dad, and that he was a member of the Three Musketeers instead of the Three Cranberries. And what would the kids in my class think when they saw those flapping lugs? What would my parents think? I mean, those things couldn't exactly be *disguised*.

But I had enough worries of my own without getting into his. The main one was putting the first lesson of the day behind me before I could sneak into the broom cupboard and home again. Unless...

Unless I could get to school before class. Getting to school before class isn't something I go out of my way to do as a rule – question of principle – but this was an emergency. I phoned the other Angie Mint to ask her to come in early with me.

'I can't,' she said. 'I'm straightening my hair.'

'Isn't it already straight?'

'It's got kinks.'

'Doesn't it usually have kinks?'

'Don't rub it in,' she said.

'I'm not rubbing anything in. I've got kinks. My hair is all kinks. I can live with them, why can't you?'

'You can live with them cos you're a boy,' she said, and hung up.

I was still standing there with the mobile in my mitt when it rang again.

'I forgot,' Angie said when I put it to my sticky-out ear. 'You're not Juggy.'

'No. So will you come to school early with me?'

'I can't. I'm straightening my hair.'

She hung up again.

At home I usually go down to breakfast in my PJs and dressing gown, but this wasn't my house any more than the school was my school and I'd have felt undressed around Golden Oldies who looked like my parents but weren't. I put on the same clothes as yesterday (because they were my own) and went downstairs. In the kitchen, the mother-who-wasn't lobbed me a big surprised smile and said how unusual it was to see me dressed before breakfast.

'Gotta go in early,' I told her. I could hardly meet her eye. Either one of them. Apart from the hair, she was a dead-ringer for my mum right down to the last varicose vein, but she wasn't her.

'Why have you got to go in early?' she asked.

My mind blanked. Best I could come up with was that one of the teachers had asked for my help before class.

'Which teacher?'

'Mr Rice.' Tragically, this was the first name that came to me.

'Oh, you'll be getting the gear ready for tomorrow then.'

'Gear ready? Tomorrow?'

'For the big weekend.'

'The big…?' With all this going on I'd forgotten the Rice Krispies Survival Weekend. So the same thing was set to occur here. There were absolutely no pluses to switching worlds. 'Yeah, that's it,' I said. 'He needs help with the gear.'

'Well, have a bowl of cereal before you go.'

'Thanks, Mum.' Smooth, eh?

'Good to see that your ears are back where they should be,' she said as I went to the cupboard where the cereals are kept at home, hoping they were also kept there here.

'Yes,' I said. 'Got me kind of worried for a minute when you said they were flat like normal people's.' The cereals were in the same place, but I couldn't find my new favourite. 'No Choco Nuggets?'

'Since when did you like chocolate cereals?' Mum 2 asked.

'Um...' Had to be careful here. 'How about always?'

'News to me,' she said. 'Whenever I've brought a chocolate cereal home you've asked me to get something healthier next time.'

'Healthier? Me?'

'Don't tell me you've gone off the Super-Nutritious All-Swiss Muesli with Extra Fruit and Vitamins.'

This caused me to lose the use of my mouth for a minute. What sort of alien language was this woman speaking? Nutritious? Muesli? Extra Fruit? Vitamins? Didn't she know her son was a teenage boy?

While I was still trying to reactivate the mouth flap, she reached past me and took out the packet of Super-Nutritious All-Swiss Muesli with Extra

Fruit and Vits and carried it to the table. She tipped a small mountain of this unnatural stuff into a bowl, went to the fridge for a carton of milk, poured some on to the stuff, and handed me a spoon.

I sat down at the table and stared into the bowl while she did other things in another part of the kitchen. I, Jiggy McCue, was expected to eat muesli? Super-Nutritious muesli? Super-Nutritious All-Swiss Muesli with Extra Fruit and Vitamins? But I had to. I didn't dare run the risk of letting her think I might not be her son. If she even suspected that, a huge round of questions might start flying. If she was like my real mum she wouldn't let me out of the door until she knew everything. School might be cancelled for the day, and that would be terrible.*

I dipped into the bowl, closed my eyes, and plunged the loaded spoon into my muesli hole. My mouth was immediately full of sawdust, wood chippings and squashed beetles. And that wasn't all.

'The milk's off,' I gasped, spitting the Swiss muck back into the bowl.

---

* I can't believe I just said that.

'It can't be,' Mum 2 said. 'I only bought it yesterday.'

But she went to the fridge and took the carton out again.

'It's nowhere near its sell-by,' she said, squinting at the small print along the top. She brought the carton to the table and showed me the date. She was right. But then I saw the printing below it.

'That's semi-skimmed soya milk.'

'Well, of course it is,' she said.

'Why have you given me semi-skimmed soya milk?

'Because it's your favourite. You wouldn't drink any other milk, you've said so many a time.'

'I have?'

'You have, Juggy. It's the healthy option, you're always saying so.'

Juggy. Of course. Different kid. But *that* different? A McCue male who was into healthy options? This other world was even more insane than I thought. But I had to cover myself.

'It could be me,' I said. 'I've been thinking for a while that maybe I don't like soya milk and muesli so much any more. Is there any bread for toast?'

'Yes, of course. But you'll have to do it yourself, I must get ready for work.'

She was on her way out of the kitchen when Dad 2 came in. They wrestled in the doorway to get past one another, then she was out and he was in.

'Hey, Jug.'

'Hey…Dad.'

He went to the bread bin and took out a loaf, sawed a couple of wedges off, dropped them in the toaster. When I saw the kind of bread it was I wasn't hungry any more. It was brown, very grainy, with loose bits on top. My real father would never have eaten bread like that. Nor would the real me. I felt in my pocket. There was some change in there. Maybe I'd get some proper food on the way to school.

Five minutes later, after going to the bathroom and cleaning my teeth with a finger like I had the night before (I wasn't using someone else's toothbrush even if his teeth were identical to mine), I was almost ready to leave. I looked in the fridge for my lunch box. Mum usually does my school lunches the night before and puts the box in the fridge, but there was no lunch box in this fridge. I went to the bottom of the stairs. It didn't feel right doing this, but I was trying to seem normal, so I yelled up.

'Mum!'

A pause.

'Mu-um!'

The bathroom door opened. She looked down.

'Yes?'

'Where's my lunch box?'

'Lunch box?'

'Yeah, where is it?'

'That's tomorrow,' she said.

'What's tomorrow?'

'When you take a lunch box.'

'What about today?'

'What do you want one today for? You did pay in your dinner money on Monday, didn't you?'

'Er…ye-es…'

What else could I say? So this Juggy character was forced to have school dinners? Poor kid. No wonder his ears stuck out.

I put on my jacket, shouted 'Bye!' to anyone

who cared, grabbed the school bag I'd brought home yesterday, and was about to close the door on myself when I heard a voice.

'Well, thank you *very* much,' it said.

I turned. Swoozie stood there in her green uniform − green for a school other than Arnold Snit Compulsory. She was frowning.

'What's up?' I asked.

'If you go back through the broom cupboard I'll never see you again,' she said. 'You know that and you don't even bother to say goodbye?'

Put like that it did sound a bit mean. Fact is, I hadn't thought of it.

'Didn't think of it,' I admitted.

'That makes it even worse,' she said.

'Sorry.'

'So you should be.'

'You want your brother back, don't you?'

'Course I do, but I thought we were friends.'

Friends. We'd only known each other since yesterday and this little girl already thought of me as a friend. Now I felt *really* bad.

'We are,' I said feebly.

'Well friends say goodbye when they're

going away,' she said.

'Yeah. Right. Bye then.'

She stuck her jaw out and scowled up at me.

'They say it *properly*.'

She reached up with both hands, grabbed my shoulders, and pulled me down to her level. Then...she kissed me, once on each cheek.

'And don't you dare forget me, Jiggy McCue!' she said, and closed the door.

Chapter Thirteen

I was just closing the front gate when I remembered that there was someone apart from Angie who might go to school early with me. I walked past the house that should be mine, trying not to look like I was peering sideways into the windows, and reached Eejit's gate.

At home, the Atkins' garden is never up to much. Mr and Mrs A are nice enough, but they don't bother with their garden at all, front or back, so imagine my surprise when I saw that these Atkins' front garden was quite well looked after. There were nice flowers, the grass was short, and there were no beer cans all over the place. In my world, the cans are lobbed by Eejit's brother Jolyon when he's finished with them. Maybe this world's Jolyon had been sent to an institution for young offenders, where he belonged.

I opened the gate, walked up the path, and rang the bell. A tall, neat person with neat hair opened the door. He wore a neat suit and tie and a really neat shirt. He smiled at me. A very neat smile.

'Hi, Jug. Early, aren't you?'

It was an almost unrecognisable Jolyon. I looked at the slice of neck above the neat collar. No barbed-wire tattoo. I looked at his hands. No H.A.T.E. on the four left fingers, no H.A.T.E. on the four right ones. Here was a Jolyon who didn't hate. A Jolyon who looked like he wouldn't bad-mouth anyone and said grace before meals. A Jolyon who didn't drink too much or hang out with other hooligans, and changed his socks every day.

'What?' he said. 'My tie crooked?'

'No, I...'

'You're early.'

Eejit, who was quite a bit smaller than his brother, had appeared in Jolyon's armpit. He was still in his pyjamas.

'That's what I said.' Still smiling neatly, Jolyon stepped back to let Eejit through.

'I want to try the broom cupboard before school,' I explained when we were alone. 'Wondered if you'd come with me.'

'Early to school?' Eejit said. It obviously wasn't something he did a lot of either. 'I'm not dressed and I'm still having my breakfast.'

'It's OK,' I said. 'Just thought I'd ask.'

'Give me ten minutes.'

'Don't worry.' I turned away. 'See you later – or not, if it works.'

He said something as I headed for the gate, but I didn't catch it.

Once the estate was behind me I saw a few other kids dawdling or playing the fool so they wouldn't get to school too soon, but none of them wore faces I knew well enough to talk to, so I didn't have to get into anything with them. I zipped through the shopping arcade and from there to school. The name on the big board attached to the fence that runs round half the school was the one Angie and Eejit had told me about. It was there yesterday, of course, but I hadn't noticed it as I was leaving. Apart from the name everything looked about the same as at Ranting Lane. There were even a couple of younger kids playing hopscotch in a corner of the playground, like there often is when I get to school. Probably dumped there by their parents on the way to work.

I didn't hang about. The odd early teacher might be behind the windows that overlook the playground. Running low (because no one notices you when you run low) I reached the double doors of the main building and pushed the bar. It didn't budge. I tried the other door, which did. I opened it a fraction and peeked in. No one beyond. I stepped inside. I closed the door by hand. If I'd just let it go, like I usually do, it would have clanged all round the building. Mr Heathcliff's broom cupboard was just around the corner up ahead, and a little way along. I trotted to the corner and peered round. The way was clear all the way to the broom cupboard, but the door was open. Heathcliff was reaching in for something.

I waited, hoping he would go. He backed out with a pair of step ladders, which he propped against the wall while he went back in for something else. This time when he came out he was holding an old tin box of tools. Oh good, I thought, he'll go now. And he did. He hoisted the ladders under his arm and walked off with the toolbox in his other hand. But not before he'd locked the door.

'Bummer,' said a voice behind me.

I whirled. 'Atkins, what are you doing here?'

'I said I'd come with you, didn't I?'

'No. You said you weren't dressed and hadn't finished your breakfast.'

'I also said I'd get a move on, but you wouldn't wait.'

'I didn't get that, I was in a hurry.'

'What for, to see Heathcliff carry a ladder down the corridor?'

'He's ruined everything,' I said.

'You mean the key thing?'

'Yes, I mean the key thing. Key things turned in lock things kind of prevent people from getting into broom cupboard things, savvy?'

'You don't have to talk to me like I'm a moron,' he said.

'I'm used to talking to you like you're a moron.'

'Well get un-used to it. I'm the best friend you have here. And I can get you into that cupboard.'

'You can? How? Got an axe or crowbar in your school bag?'

'No, something a bit more portable.'

He took a bunch of keys out of his pocket and

dangled them in my face.

'You think one of those'll fit the lock?' I said.

'Sure of it.'

When we reached the broom cupboard, Atkins inspected the lock, then started going through the keys. 'Keep a lookout,' he whispered.

'Lookout?' I said. 'We're in the middle of a corridor that goes both ways. At the end of both ways there's a corner. I can only keep a lookout at one of those corners, and I'm not at either of them.'

'So keep a lookout both ways.'

'But what if a teacher or someone comes?'

'Then you tell me.'

'I won't need to tell you. They'll have seen us by then.'

He glared at me. 'D'you want my help or don't you?'

'Course I want your help. I'm just stating the obvious, that's all.'

'Well don't.'

He slotted one of the keys in the lock and turned it, but not far.

'Doesn't work,' I said.

He tried another key. Same result.

'Still no good,' I said.

He glared at me again.

'I'm just saying that it's another wrong key,' I said.

'I know that.'

'So why use it?'

'I didn't know till I tried it. I won't know which key fits till it turns the lock.'

'What makes you think any of them will turn it?'

'They're skeleton keys. I just have to find the right one.'

'What are you doing with skeleton keys?'

'They're my dad's.'

'What's your dad doing with skeleton keys?'

He put another key in. 'Not a lot since they caught him.'

'Who caught him?'

'The police.'

'Caught him what?'

'Breaking and entering.'

'Breaking and…?'

He tried a fourth key. 'The chemists in the shopping arcade. He spray-painted the CCTV-cam but the lens had been treated with an anti-spray agent, so they were still able to record his every movement.'

'Hold on,' I said. 'Are you saying your dad's a burglar?'

'No, I'm saying he's a guest of His Majesty's Prison Service.' He took the fourth useless key out of the lock. 'Hey,' he said. 'If my family lives next door to you in your world and your Eejit's dad's line of work isn't common knowledge, he must still be free there.'

'He is. We thought Mr Atkins was a landscape gardener who didn't bring his work home.'

'Well, if he's still free when you get back, you could warn him to steer clear of the shopping centre cameras.'

'Oh sure. I'll ring his doorbell one evening and say, "Listen, Mr Atkins, whatever you do when you break into another shop, choose one that's not near any cameras."'

Eejit shoved another key in the lock. Yet another that might as well have been a chocolate éclair for all the good it did.

'I thought skeleton keys fitted every lock,' I said.

He sorted through the bunch of keys again. 'You

thought wrong. You need a good range to cover every kind of lock. One of these'll do it.'

He tried another key. And...

'And there we are,' he said.

He turned the doorknob. The door opened.

'Hello, what are you two up to?'

We turned. It was Mr Rice. The other Mr Rice. The one who lived in the house that should have been mine. And he was coming towards us.

Chapter Fourteen

At first, I thought that the other Mr Rice was like my Mr Rice in every way except the way he dressed. Like I said back there somewhere, the Mr Rice I know is never seen without his red tracksuit. Just as well if it's the only thing he owns, I suppose, but this one wasn't wearing a red tracksuit. He was wearing a saggy red romper suit that he might have picked up at a Teletubbies' car boot sale. 'Does he always dress like that?' I asked Atkins as the other Mr Rice came towards us. He didn't answer. Too busy closing the door, fiddling with the keys behind his back, and trying to look like his halo would be delivered by courier any minute.

'What's so darned fascinating about Mr Heathcliff's hidey-hole?' Mr Rice asked as he joined us.

'Jug and I were just saying that you'd think he'd wipe the grubby marks off his door seeing as he's the caretaker,' Eejit said.

Mr Rice held out one of his enormous palms. 'May I see?'

'See what, Coach?'

'Whatever it is you have behind your back.'

'Behind my back? The only thing behind my back is the door.'

'Well in that case you won't mind showing me, will you?'

'No problem,' Eejit stepped aside so Rice could see the door better.

'I mean your hands, Ralph.'

'Oh, my *hands*,' Eejit said.

He held out one of his hands. It was empty.

'And the other one?'

He showed his other hand. Also empty.

Mr Rice grinned. 'I pulled the same trick when I was your age.'

'Trick, sir?'

Mr Rice reached behind Eejit's collar. 'Always keep your keys here, do you?' he said, lifting out the bunch.

Atkins smiled. Fair cop. 'Doesn't everyone?'

'I'll hang on to them for now,' Rice said. 'Collect

them from the staff room at the end of the day. Now, outside, the pair of you.'

'He didn't shout,' I said to Atkins as we went.

'Why would he shout?'

'Well, my Mr Rice always shouts, whether you've done something wrong or not.'

'Really? Ours doesn't. Not often. He's OK, Mr Rice.'

'So what do we do now?' I said when we were outside again.

'About what?' said Atkins.

'About getting into the broom cupboard.'

'Have to try again at morning break.'

'We won't have your keys at morning break.'

'Maybe it won't be locked then. Mr Heathcliffs obviously don't always lock their doors or you wouldn't be here now.'

'Yes. Curse them.'

We hung around the playground while it slowly filled up with kids. When Angie arrived with her straightened hair, she didn't spend much time with us because she had stuff to talk about with some girls. That was almost as weird as Mr Rice not shouting or wearing a tracksuit. My Angie prefers to hang out with the boys and agrees with me and Pete that she was short-changed when she got the female bits instead of our manly gear. But this Angie was different. She seemed to actually like being female! Even in school uniform she looked more girlie than my Angie ever did in anything. As well as her hair, she'd taken trouble with the way her face looked, and her nails were neatly filed and polished, and she walked like she had books on her head. She even had bigger chest bumps, so I guessed she'd discovered inflatable bras. If my Angie ever wore one of those I'd have to stick a pin in it. Two pins.

The first lesson of the day turned out to be Highland Dancing with Mrs Porterhouse. Yes, Highland Dancing. In the real world, my world, Mrs Porterhouse teaches Geography. I guessed that this Mrs P did too, only she'd decided to liven the subject up a bit, like my Mrs P does occasionally without any success whatever. Highland Dancing, though? We were nowhere near any highlands. But maybe you had to be trained in it at school here because when you grew up you were expected to Highland Dance every weekend instead of download music and anything else you can think of. Perhaps adults here Highland Danced every free hour of their stupid lives until it was time to apply for the Zimmer.

I stuck my hand up. 'Miss!'

'Yes, Juggy?'

'Miss, can't we just do Geography?'

'Geography?'

'Yes. Can't we be bored out of our cranial cavities with that instead of poncing about to the sound of squealing cats?'

'Well, you could if I actually *took* Geography,' she chirruped. 'Come on, Juggy, you did very well last week.'

'I did?'

'You know you did. You're a natural dancer. Why else would I have asked you to show the others how it was done?'

So this Mrs Porterhouse didn't teach Geography, and Juggy McCue was the High King of Highland Dancing. I had to be careful not to say the wrong thing here.

'Miss, can you answer another question for me?'

'If I can, certainly.'

'Can you tell me what use Highland Dancing is to anyone with a single brain cell left who doesn't live in the Highlands or wear a kilt?'

This seemed to floor her a bit. 'Well,' she said after a pause, 'you never know when you'll be called upon to do it, I suppose.'

'I do,' I said. 'Never.'

'There's always the off-chance, Juggy.'

'Yeah, well off-chances don't usually come in bundles, miss. Maybe you never noticed that.'

'The fact remains,' she said more firmly, 'that we'll be doing Highland Dancing every Friday till the end of term as part of the government's Physical Activity Nurtured Through Schools initiative.'

'You're teaching Highland Dancing for the whole term?' I gasped.

'It's only one period a week,' she replied. Then she grinned brightly all around. 'Next term, we'll be getting into shape with something rather different. We'll be studying Liposuction, Face-lifting and Body-hair Sculpture. Won't that be exciting?'

Damn. And I was going to miss it.

We spent the five or six years till morning break with our knees and arms in the air, hopping from one toe to the other to avoid plastic swords while the Porterhouse played shrieky bagpipes through the speakers of her tiny eardrum-busting music machine. When this ordeal was over and we'd Highland Danced out of her presence, I had just twenty minutes to get into Mr Heathcliff's broom cupboard and not come out again. Angie knew what I planned to do, so she didn't go off with her girlie chums this time, but loitered with Eejit and me as close to the broom cupboard as we could get while we waited for the corridor to empty. I started this loiter with a grumble.

'Dunno why we're standing here. Might as well go outside and make daisy-chains or draw something rude on a wall.'

'Why?' said Atkins.

'It'll be locked. That's the way my luck goes. And Mr Rice took your skeleton keys.'

'I've got it covered,' he said.

'Got what covered?'

'If you remember, the door was unlocked when I handed over the keys.'

'Yes, but Heathcliff's bound to have been back and locked it again since then.'

'Maybe, maybe not.'

When the corridor emptied we snuck to the broom cupboard. I turned the handle. 'Told you,' I said when the door didn't open.

'Try this,' said Eejit, opening his hand. There was a key in it.

'Where'd you get that?'

He popped the key into the lock, turned it, opened the door a tad.

'It's the one I used earlier.'

'It can't be. It was on the ring Mr Rice confiscated.'

'I slipped it off before he took it.'

'I didn't see you do that.'

'You were beside me, not behind my back where the action was.'

'He's good at sleight-of-hand,' Angie said. 'Comes of having a burglar in the family.'

'My dad prefers Private Entry Executive,' Eejit said. 'But yes, I've learnt a lot from him. If I don't make it to Uni at least I'll never starve, thanks to all the stuff Dad's shown me.' He held the door open for me. 'Over to you.'

I stepped inside a little way. 'Hola, hola, hola,' I said in parting.

'One for all and all for one,' Angie replied.

'Lunch,' I said.

'What?'

'It's "one for all and all for lunch".'

'Oh yeah. Shows how memorable it is, doesn't it?'

I closed the door on them. The smell of polish and dust and caretakery sweat hit me as I felt my way through the deep darkness. I wasn't sure how it worked, but I imagined I'd have to go right through this cupboard to get to the door of the Ranting Lane one. My left foot touched something. I reached down. It was the tripping bucket. I made my way round the bucket before standing up straight again – and banged my shoulder on a shelf. I knew it was a shelf because something about the size of a tin of polish fell off it and cracked me on the side of the head on its way to the floor. I kicked it aside and carried on groping forward, wishing I'd thought to turn the light on – the switch

163

was probably just inside the door – because in darkness that lightless I couldn't tell how far it was to the back. I felt my way round boxes and pots and things, bumped into a chair, fingered the smelly old workcoats, and after a while touched something flat that had to be a door. I felt for a handle, and found one. I turned it, opened the door, and blinked at the light of a school corridor just like the one I'd left a few minutes before.

I'd made it! I was back where I belonged!

As I stepped out of the broom cupboard, a voice said, 'Hello! You, lad! What business do you have in there?'

It was Mother Hubbard, Ranting Lane's beloved Head. I closed the door with relief as he came towards me.

'Looking for Mr Heathcliff, sir.'

'Why, pray?'

'Why pray?' I said. 'My dad's always saying that. Prayers are a waste of time, he says. Never work for him.'

Mr H frowned. 'Are you trying to be funny?' he asked sternly.

As he said this my eyes drifted down to the left lapel of his jacket, and a little badge shaped like a volcano.

I was still at Arnold Snit Compulsory!

Chapter Fifteen

I was pretty fed up when I joined Eejit and Angie in the playground. They didn't get it right away because the wads of chewing gum were still behind my ears. Eejit held his hand up to be slapped.

'Good to have you back, Cavaleiro!'

I didn't slap it. Wouldn't have been time anyway, because Angie jumped between us and threw her arms round my neck.

'We thought we'd lost you!' she squealed girlishly.

'Wish you had,' I said, spitting straightened hair out of my mouth. 'Dump the hugs, willya? I have rules about this stuff.'

She let go of me with a puzzled expression. Obviously, hugs weren't off-limits between the Three Carveries.

'What was it like there?' Eejit asked.

'It's a broom cupboard,' I said sourly. 'What do you think it was like?'

'I mean in Jiggy's world.'

'Fantastic. Oceans better than here.'

This seemed to interest him. 'In what way?'

'In every way,' I snapped.

He frowned up at me. 'What happened?'

'Take a flying guess.'

'It's not him,' said Angie. She'd gone round the back of me to check the lug supports. 'He's still the pathetic copy.'

Atkins gaped. 'But he went into the broom cupboard!'

'And came out again.'

'You turned round and came straight out again?' he said to me.

'No, I didn't turn round and come straight out again. It was too dark to go straight in any direction.'

'But you must have known which way you were going.'

'I did, but something fell on me, obviously threw me off course.'

'Well, why didn't you turn the light on?'

'I didn't think of it till it was too late.'

He groaned. 'You're really brilliant, aren't you?'

It wasn't a compliment.

'You'll have to try again at lunchtime,' said Angie.

'Same thing might happen then,' I mumbled.

'Don't be so defeatist. You won't know till you try.'

'And if I fail again?'

'You try again after school if there's no one about.'

'And if there is someone about?'

'You try again on Monday.'

'Monday? A whole Survival Weekend away?'

'Survival Weekend?'

'The legendary Jiggy McCue sense of humour,' Atkins muttered.

'It'll be a very interesting weekend,' Angie said.

'For you maybe,' I said. 'You're not stuck in the wrong world, wrong house, with the wrong friends, wrong parents, and a sister.'

'What's wrong with Swoozie?'

'Nothing's wrong with Swoozie. Swoozie's OK. I'm just saying.'

Angie came to stand in front of me. She looked serious.

'You want to count yourself lucky you've got us,' she said. 'You want to also count yourself lucky that we believe you're who you say you are.'

'You have to,' I said, and waggled my ears. One of the blobs of gum fell out. I picked it up, licked the dirt off, stuck it back.

'On top of that you want to count yourself lucky we're prepared to go out of our way to help you,' she said.

'Some help,' I grouched. 'I'm still here, aren't I?'

'Eej,' she said to Atkins. 'I don't think we're appreciated here.'

'I think you're right,' he said.

With that, they span round and walked away. I watched them go, feeling suddenly very friendless. And lonely.

When I saw Pete Garrett across the playground I suddenly wanted to talk to him. Garrett had been there to chew the cud with and give Chinese burns to all my life. I needed that right now. He wasn't with Skinner this time, he was with Sami Safadi and Milo Dakin. That wasn't so bad. Sami and Milo are OK in my world. I went over.

'Hey,' I said.

'Hey, Jug,' said Milo.

'Hey, Jug,' said Sami.

'Hey, Pete,' I repeated to the one who hadn't answered.

He scowled at me. 'What do you want?'

'Want? I don't want anything. Being friendly, is all.'

'Friendly? We're not friends, McCue. Never will be.'

That hurt. My lifelong bud Pete Garrett was telling me he wasn't my friend. I know he wasn't actually my Pete, but he was the nearest thing to him that there was around here. Garrett and I had fallen out occasionally, but we'd known one another longer than anyone except Angie because our three mothers were in each other's houses from day one until his mum legged it with the podium-dancing osteopath with Tourette's and his dad moved in with Angie's mother Audrey.

'Give us a minute, willya?' I said to Sami and Milo.

'What for?' Sami asked.

'Wanna talk to Garrett.'

'What do you want to talk to me about?' Pete said suspiciously.

'I'll tell you when these two put a couple of gaps between us.'

'We have nothing to say to one another.'

'We might have.'

'We haven't, McCue. We haven't had anything to say to one another since we were six. Now get away from me. Scoot.'

He sounded like he meant it. Looked it too. I scooted. Sadly. Thought I heard him and the others chuckling as I went.

It was a long morning. Longer than most because it was History with Hurley, which I could certainly have done without. They must have had a different timetable there, because by Friday at Ranting Lane History's behind us. This Mr Hurley wasn't as cheerful as mine the last time I saw him either. He didn't crack a smile once, so I guessed he had no immediate plans to bore people senseless on a cruise ship. He spent the whole period writing stuff about some industrial resolution on the board for us to copy down and memorise because he'd be testing us next week.

I hoped he wouldn't be testing me next week.

Atkins sat next to me, like he had in Spiritual Technology. Maybe he sat next to me in most lessons, the way Pete did at home, but he didn't seem to want to talk to me to fight the boredom, like Pete would. I didn't make any effort to talk to him either. If he and the other Angie Mint were going to be like that, I could be like it too.

But then it was lunchtime. Time for another stab at the broom cupboard. Only trouble was...

'Atkins,' I whispered as we packed up at the end of the lesson.

He put a hand to his ear, like someone listening for distant thunder.

'Did I hear my name spoken by some complete stranger who doesn't value the few friends he has?'

'I need the key,' I said.

He stuffed his books into his bag. 'What key?'

'The one we opened the broom cupboard with earlier. Did you take it out of the lock when I went in?'

'Maybe I did, maybe I didn't,' he said, moving away.

'If I don't get in,' I said, a bit louder so others could hear, 'you'll never get your pal back.'

He stopped. Came back. Hissed at me.

'That's blackmail.'

'It's not blackmail, it's a fact. You want him back or don't you?'

'Given the choice between him and you? Hmm, tough one.'

He dipped into his pocket, handed me the key, and was about to leave when I asked him something that had been bothering me since morning break.

'Have you got any idea why Pete Garrett doesn't like Juggy?'

'Sure,' he said. 'Common knowledge.'

'Not to me.'

'Until they were six, the two of them were best pals. Then, one day when they were playing marbles in the playground, they got into a scrap about who had the best marbles and Jug dropped Garrett's down a drain.'

'And that's it?'

'Garrett was very proud of those marbles.'

'Well, he's not the only one who's lost his

173

marbles round here.'

Atkins shoved off.

Desperate as I was to get back to my proper world and my true friends, it was that time of day when chow is wolfed, and I was hungry. I didn't have my usual packed lunch, but the mother-who-wasn't had asked me if her son had paid his dinner money in, which must mean he was entitled to eat in the canteen. I'd never stayed for school dinners at Ranting Lane. Nor had Pete and Angie. Packed lunches in the Concrete Garden, that was our routine. We preferred it that way. More freedom.

Even if the canteen had been in a different part of the building here, I would have known where it was because half the school was scrambling in a direction that wasn't the playground. I didn't have time to go with the flow and saunter at slug speed towards the dishing-up counters while kids with an hour to kill tried to decide whether to have the beans or the chips. I pushed my way through the crowd, stuck elbows in ribs, took every short cut in town, and when the canteen doors were opened I was among the first eleven food disciples.

'How'd you get up there, McCue?' a voice rang out.

'Cos I'm quick, Ryan,' I shouted back.

'I never noticed before,' he replied.

'That's because you're so slow, bung-head.'

'Watch it McCue.'

'Watch it yourself, Ryan.'

I couldn't believe what I saw when I got to the row of food counters. At Ranting Lane they serve the chips and burgers and sausages and stuff that packed lunchers aren't allowed near. Here there wasn't a chip or burger or sausage in sight. It was all pasta and salad and vegetables and rice with bits in. The sort of low-fat chow that would make my dad turn in his grave if he was dead. I almost turned in my own and went off to starve in the broom cupboard, but then I thought, 'Suppose I don't make it past the brooms again and I stay stuck here? I'll starve all afternoon.' Better to shove a spoonful of school pasta down me than shove nothing at all. I could always close my eyes and hold my nose.

So that's what I did, except for the eye-closing and nose-holding. I even had a little bowl of fruit salad afterwards so all the gaps would be filled. I wolfed the whole lot in five minutes flat. I sat on my own while I did this. I didn't want to talk to anyone. These weren't kids I knew. Even faces that I could draw on the back of someone's hand didn't belong to people I knew.

I was just jamming the last organic pineapple chunk in my trap when I caught Pete Garrett's eye. I forgot for a sec that we weren't friends here and raised my hand. Maybe if the pineapple chunk hadn't just found a parking place behind my teeth I might have thrown him a friendly grin as well, but a grin wasn't possible without firing the p. chunk at Gemma Kausa and Holly Gilder on the next table. It could be that because of the grin famine my raised hand didn't look so much like a friendly greeting, because the hand Garrett raised in reply was definitely not.

From the canteen I zipped to the corridor where the broom cupboard was. A couple of lady teachers were chatting near it. I went past them and loitered just round the corner, constantly looking back to see if they'd gone yet. After a while, when it started to look like they'd be there till Doomsday – they were in full-frontal natter mode – I went back to them.

'Scuse me, Miss,' I said, meaning both of them at once. You can't really say 'Scuse me, Misses'.

They stopped speaking. Asked me what I wanted.

'Some trouble in the playground,' I lied with a worried expression.

'What kind of trouble?'

'You have to see it. Some kids over the far side.'

'I'll attend to it,' one of them said to the other, and she stormed in the direction of the playground.

I followed her, slowly, until, glancing back, I saw the other teacher go off in the opposite direction and disappear round the corner. I returned to the broom cupboard and tried the handle. The door opened. Great, no need for the key after all. I'd jumped inside and closed the door before I realised the light was on.

'Help you?'

Mr Heathcliff was in there, chomping on a sandwich in a deckchair and drawing moustaches on the faces above the bosoms and bottoms in his favourite paper.

'Sorry,' I said. 'Wrong door.'

I went out again.

Things just were *not* going my way!

Chapter Sixteen

Eejit and Angie eyed me with a mixture of hope and suspicion as I walked over to them towards the end of lunch. As I still hadn't removed the gum from behind my ears they had to ask which McCue I was. When I told them about the latest failed attempt their faces sagged.

The next lesson turned out to be Science. The science teacher at Ranting Lane was Mr Flowerdew, but at Arnold Snit Compulsory it was a bloke called Mr Numnuts. I asked Eejit behind my hand if that was his real name. He said he wasn't sure, but Mr N was such a character that he wouldn't put it past him to call himself that for a joke.

Mr Numnuts wasn't all that ancient by Golden Oldie standards, about thirty maybe, and he had a pointy little beard that he'd dyed bright green, and a mass of curly hair that he hadn't. He wore this suit that was too small for him – a hairy fawn thing – and he had the tiniest feet I ever saw on someone over eight years old. Eejit said that Mr Numnuts liked to make Science fun. He told me that at the end of one lesson he filled a white balloon with hydrogen and let it float to the ceiling, then lit this long taper and touched the balloon with it. There was this ffffffffffft sound, then the balloon exploded. Everybody jumped like maniacs, and then all these little bits of white rubber drifted down like snowflakes. 'What was that for?' someone gasped. 'I just wanted to end the lesson with a bang,' said Mr Numnuts.

The science lesson I had with Mr Numnuts started out like any other – pretty dull – but once he'd run through the heavy stuff he took a small box out of the bag he'd brought with him. He didn't have a leather briefcase like most teachers. He had a big green canvas bag with the words WHY DO THE WEIRDOES ALWAYS SIT NEXT TO ME? on the side. The box he took out of the bag contained Turkish Delight, twenty pink cubes and twenty blue ones, all covered in this sugary coating that made every tongue immediately jerk out and lick lips.

'Ooh, is that for us, sir?' someone asked.

'Gordon,' he replied, unwrapping the box. He liked the kids to call him Gordon. 'And it is for you, but not to eat.'

'Can we have some anyway?'

'You can have a nibble in a minute if you're still up for it, after we've conducted our little experiment.'

'What's the experiment, Gordon?'

'Well, there'll be two. It's a comparison thing.'

He'd also brought along a pair of small transparent boxes. He put the blue cubes in one of these, which he called Group B (for blue), and the pink cubes in the other box (Group P). Then he told us to spit on the Group P cubes.

'Spit on them, sir?'

'Yes, spit on them, and will you *please* call me Gordon, I can't get be doing with all this "sir" stuff. I want you to drench every pink cube with phlegm, saliva, sputum, or whatever you want to call it.'

'What happens then?'

'Then we turn to the blue Turkish Delight.'

'And spit on that too?'

'No, we'll do something different with Group B.

181

Now gather round and get ready to hurl. Have to get a move on because we've wasted so much of this lesson on National Curriculum bilge and the bell'll go any minute.'

'Do we all have to spit, Gordon?'

'No, Julia. Only those who'd like to.'

'Only my nan says spitting's rude.'

'So it is, unless it's part of a supervised experiment by a qualified science teacher who plays keyboards in a rock band at weekends. Now gather round, those of you who want to participate.'

So we gathered round the box of pink cubes, hawked for an Oscar, and spat. Mostly it was the boys who did this. Julia Frame wasn't the only girl who stood back with a sour expression. We spat and spat and spat until all the cubes of pink Turkish Delight were dripping and shiny. When we were all spat out, Mr Numnuts put the lid on the box and we wiped our chins and grinned at one another. You don't get permission to gob your guts out in many lessons.

'Why did we have to spit on the pink Turkish Delight?' Angie asked.

'You mean why the pink instead of the blue?' said Mr Numnuts.

'Yes.'

'Worry not, Angie, it's not a gender issue. We could have spat on the blue cubes just as well.'

Someone asked what we had to do with the blue cubes.

'We're going to drench them with urine,' Mr Numnuts said.

'Urine, sir?'

'Urine, widdle, piddle, wee, pee, take your pick.'

'I'll start if you like, Gord,' said Ryan.

'Start what?'

'The spraying.'

'No need, I've come prepared. Put it away please, Bryan.'

He dipped into his WHY DO THE WEIRDOES ALWAYS SIT NEXT TO ME? bag and took out a bottle of yellow stuff.

'Sir, that isn't what I think it is…?'

'Yes, Pete, the very liquid.'

'Is it… yours?'

'No, I paid some homeless people to fill it for me. Who wants to be mother?'

'I'll do it!' said Eejit.

'I think our friend's taking the piss,' Mr N said, handing him the bottle.

When Eejit dribbled the bladder-dew over Group B there were quite a few groans, but most of us — even the girls — leaned forward to see what happened to the cubes. We were disappointed. The sugar coating cracked here and there and tried to dissolve, but that was it.

'Now what?' we asked.

'Now the bell goes,' Mr Numnuts said. (It just had.) 'And we gather here this time next week to see what's happened to the cubes over the past seven days. I'll put the boxes in this cupboard and hope Queenie doesn't come across them.* If she finds them she'll probably think we're breeding a rare form of intelligent school life and dump them. Oh — anyone fancy that nibble before we go?'

No one did.

We were about to leave when the door opened and Mr Rice looked in. He still wore the saggy red romper suit.

'May I have a word, Mr Numnuts?' he said.

'Have as many as you like as long as it's not with

---

* I found out later that Queenie was Mrs Sidaj, head cleaning lady at Arnold Snit Compulsory. I've no idea who runs the cleaning at Ranting Lane, but here it was Queenie Sidaj. Eejit told me that they called her Queenie because she acted like she ran the joint. No one — even the teachers, he said — dared cross Queenie Sidaj.

me,' Mr N replied. 'I have an appointment with a bungee-jumping instructor.'

Mr Rice looked impressed. 'You're doing bungee-jumping?'

'No, I just have an appointment with her.' Mr Numnuts grabbed his WHY DO THE WEIRDOES ALWAYS SIT NEXT TO ME? bag and waggled his hips at us. 'She's rather lovely.'

When he'd gone, Mr Rice closed the door so we couldn't escape till he said so. 'I hope the two team members in this class have been training hard for the big weekend,' he said.

'Sure have, Coach,' said Atkins.

'Good. Because I for one would love to see that trophy in a bullet-proof glass cabinet in the main hall for the next twelve months. We all would, I'm sure.'

A rumble of agreement from a few kids.

'And those of you accompanying the team, I want you to give your full support during their heats. That's why you're going, remember, to cheer them on, not to stand around observing quietly. Understood?'

Another rumble of agreement, then he said that

that was all and that we could go. As I walked past him, he touched me on the shoulder.

'Juggy.'

I paused. '…Yes?'

'I'm counting on you most of all.'

'Eh?'

What was the big wazoo on about? Since when did a Mr Rice count on a J. McCue for anything?

'Whether we bring that trophy home or not could be your call.'

'Mine?'

'Just do your very best when the time comes – OK?'

'Riiiiight,' I said, and skidded out the door.

What had a trophy to do with a Survival Weekend, for Pete's sake? Or even Eejit's sake? And why was he counting on me? Juggy, I mean. Not that I really cared. I wouldn't be Surviving with him. I'd be back in my own mad world, with my own Mr Rice, probably hiding behind a tree hoping he'd forget I existed.

Eejit and Angie went with me to the broom cupboard. There were still a few kids in the corridor, so they covered me while I tried the door.

It was locked. I popped the skeleton key in, turned it, and opened the door just enough to slip in sideways.

'In case I don't see you again...' I said to the other two of The Four.

'Yeah, yeah,' said Atkins, turning away.

'Just go,' said Angie.

This time I flipped the light switch before closing the door. It seemed so much smaller in there when you could see everything. I stepped round the tripping bucket, avoided Heathcliff's deckchair, didn't knock anything off a shelf, and in a stride or two was parting the old brown workcoats to see what was behind them. What was behind them was a wall. I pushed at the wall. It was solid. Brick solid.

Puzzle. What had been different that first time? All I could remember doing was darting into the Ranting Lane broom cupboard and walking out of the Arnie Snit Compulsory version. Oh, wait. Of course. Juggy had been in there too, on his way to my world. So did that mean that we always had to be there at the same time to swap places? If that was the case, it might never happen again. When I thought about it, it was pretty amazing that we'd gone into our respective school broom cupboards at the same time once. To do it twice would be stretching coincidence to ripping point.

Unlikely as it was that Juggy would go into the Ranting Lane broom cupboard a second time while I was there, I hung in there, hoping – until the knocks on the door started. At first I thought it was him trying to get in, but then I heard the door on the other side of the workcoats open and looked through to see Eejit and Angie peering in.

'How's it going?' one of them asked.

'It's not.'

'Still you then, are you?'

'Yeah, sorry.'

We might have talked some more, but they closed the door suddenly and I heard them answering the questions of some nosy teacher who'd charged onto the scene. Then a little rap of fingernails told me they'd been moved along. I waited a minute before cracking the door. The corridor was deserted. I slipped out and locked up after me. That was it then. I was going to be stuck here till Monday, which meant that I'd have to go on the Survival Weekend with the wrong Mr Rice after all.

Hallay-flaming-looyah.

Chapter Seventeen

At the end of the afternoon, Eejit collected the rest of his keys from Mr Rice in the staff room and the three of us started for home. (That's Eejit, me and Angie, not Eejit, me and Mr Rice.) Just before we reached the estate I told them to go on without me.

'Why, where are you going?'

'Nowhere. Just don't want to go home yet.'

'Because it's not your home exactly?'

'Probably.'

'It's somewhere to sleep,' said Angie.

'I'm not tired.'

'And eat.'

'Not hungry.'

I walked off, dragging the school bag that wasn't mine.

I didn't pay much attention to where I went. Vaguely noticed a boarded-up café, a vandalised Age Concern shop, The Jacqueline Wilson Tattoo Parlour, and that was about it. There weren't many differences between this town and mine, but I didn't need to remind myself that however familiar everything looked I'd never seen it before. I felt pretty helpless actually. Pretty hopeless. I needed my friends. My real friends. But there were no Musketeers here to gallop to the rescue at the punch of some buttons. I was absolutely alone.

'Hi, kid, how ya doin'?'

'Eh?'

I'd been mooching with my eyes on the pavement. I looked up. It was Pete Garrett's dad.

'Hi, Ollie,' I said.

He screwed his eyes up. 'Do I know you?'

I mentally slapped myself round the face, twice. The sight of him had thrown me. I'd known this man all my life. I was round his house all the time with Pete and Angie. He'd even been on holiday with us. But this wasn't the Oliver Garrett I knew. He looked a lot rougher than my Oliver, couldn't have shaved for days, there were bags under his eyes, and his hair was long and greasy.

'I'm a friend of Pete's,' I said. Well, it was partly true.

I realised where we were. *The King's Arms* pub. Except it wasn't called *The King's Arms* here. The old wooden sign swinging high up on the wall told me that in this wonky world it was called *The Queen's Legs*.

'Got any money?' the other Oliver Garrett asked.

So that was why he'd called to me.

'Money? No. Sorry.'

I had a few coins in my pocket, but I might need them. I started to go. But then I felt guilty about leaving him there without saying something friendly. He might not be the Ollie I knew, but he was sort of the same person, and he looked like he might be glad of a spot of lively conversation.

'What are you up to then?' I asked with a friendly smile.

'Up to?'

'I mean what are you doing?'

'Doing?' He scowled. 'Whatja think I'm doing? I'm waiting for *The Queen's Legs* to open so I can get a drink.'

I moved on.

Eventually I had to admit I was a bit peckish. I took another route to the estate, and as I still didn't have a front door key, went round the back of the house that wasn't mine. I opened the gate – cautiously – and peeked round the fence. Stallone the dog stuck his snout out of the kennel and started towards me with a growl. I jumped back, slammed the gate, and went round to the front to wait for Juggy's mum or dad to get home from work. I flopped down on the step, wishing I'd stashed some chocolate bars or crisps in the bag I'd been dragging round all day.

'Joseph?'

I hadn't heard the door open behind me. I turned. Swoozie.

'No,' I said.

'Are you sure?' she asked, looking me in the ears.

'If you mean your brother, yeah, definitely sure.'

'Didn't you go back into the broom cupboard?'

'Three times,' I said. 'Didn't work once.'

'Oh dear. But why are you sitting on the step?'

'Because I didn't think anyone was in.'

'I'm always in by this time. I go to my friend Penny's for half an hour after school and come home when I know you're in. I mean when Joseph's in. But no one was in today.'

'So how did you get in?'

'With the key under the front step.'

'Your mum puts a back door key under the front step?'

'A front door key. In case Joseph's late.'

'My mum doesn't put any kind of key under the front step,' I said.

'You don't have a sister,' said Swoozie.

She was right, I didn't have a sister, but now that I thought of it, if my mum had put a front door key under the front step when we moved to the Brook Farm Estate instead of a back door key up the garden gnome's bum, I could have got in so much more easily all this time.

I went into the house. Swoozie closed the door.

'Sorry to disappoint you,' I said.

'Disappoint me?'

'Not being your brother.'

'Well, I expect we'll get him back sooner or later,' she said. 'And it's nice to have you here.'

'You're just saying that.'

She beamed me a colossal smile that told me that she wasn't just saying it, she really meant it. Then she gripped one of my elbows and pulled me into the kitchen.

'Bet you're hungry,' she said.

'How'd you guess?'

'You're a growing boy. Shall I make you a Vegemite sandwich?'

'No, I'll just have a batch of bickies.'

She got out the biscuit tin and opened it for me. I grabbed a handful.

'Better?' she said when I'd rammed half of them past my teeth.

'Yeah.'

'Got any homework?'

'Homework? Should I have?'

'Sometimes Joseph does, sometimes he doesn't. I help him with it. Well, I do most of it really. He just copies it out.'

'Get away. You're too young for a thirteen year old's homework.'

She beamed again. 'Young but bright.'

'Brighter than him?'

'No, it's just that I like doing homework and he doesn't. In return he makes my bed and stuff.'

'He makes your bed?'

'Yes. He's so much better at bed-making than I am.'

'But – but – but he's a boy!' I stammered.

'He's my brother,' said Swoozie happily. 'He loves me.'

That evening I picked up some more weird info about this world. Not only did Juggy make his own bed and his sister's, but his dad did most of the cooking, washing, vacuuming, and just about every other thing that my mum complains about doing without help. He wasn't the only dad either. Housework was Man's Work here. And what did the women do? The women earned the big money, checked the oil and tyres of the cars, and went to football matches. Yep. Went to football. And the football was played by…women!

I got most of this from Swoozie, but one piece of news came from her dad after he'd loaded the dishwasher following the meal he cooked when he got in from work.

'Better get one last practice in, Jug,' he said.

'Practice?'

'Come on, let's see how you do.'

He took the ironing board from its cupboard and

set it up in the kitchen. While the iron was warming up he brought a big plastic basket in. The basket contained a heap of clothes he'd put through the washing machine and tumble dryer last night or the night before.

'What do you want to try first?' he asked.

'First?'

'Shirt, trousers, pants?'

'You choose.'

'OK, let's ease into it with your mother's undies.'

He found a pair of little blue things and laid them out on the ironing board. Then we both stood there looking at them like we were waiting for them to get up and dance.

'Go on then,' Dad 2 said. 'The iron should be warm enough by now.'

I stared. At the pants. At him. At the pants again. 'You want me to iron these things?'

'Of course.' When I went right on staring at them, he laughed. 'Come on, son, you want to win that trophy, don't you?'

'Trophy?'

He closed my fingers round the handle of the iron. He actually expected me to press his wife's knickers. And because I had to act like he thought I would, I bit the bullet, spat it out, and got stuck in.

But after a few seconds he asked why I was doing it like that.

'Like what?'

'Well, the way you're going about it, you'd think you'd never ironed women's underwear before.'

'Oh, really?'

'Stretch that section between your thumb and fingers and ease the point of the iron in. That's it. Don't press, the iron'll do that. Just ease it in and follow the contour... yes... and withdraw, and go smoothly over the stern... oh, that's more like it.' He chuckled. 'Had me worried there, lad!'

After the little knickers I had to iron the other clothes in the basket, clothe after clothe. Just as well my mother had given me that bit of tutoring a couple of nights back or I'd have been really stuck. I think I did a pretty neat job actually. My real father would have been ashamed of me.

I'd just ironed the last thing in the basket when Swoozie's mother wandered in.

'How did he do?' she asked her husband.

'He's done better. Still, I guess it won't be about quality so much as content.' He looked at me. 'Feel like going to hang upside down from a tree in the park?'

Mum 2 got in before I could get my lips round an answer to this.

'He's put in enough practice over the past few weeks, Mel. He'll either do well at the weekend or he won't. It's in the lap of the gods.'

'Or Xenu,' said Dad 2 with a sigh.

'What he needs is an early night, to be fresh for tomorrow. Go on, Juggy, up you go, get a good night's sleep.'

'But it's only nine o'clock,' I said.

'Yes,' she said. 'And you're about to pass the watershed. Upstairs.'

I didn't dare appear too clueless, so up I went.

Swoozie's light was on. I knocked on her door.

'Come in, Joseph.'

I looked in. 'Your parents are insane,' I said.

'Bit heavy with the ironing practice, were they?'

'A bit and a half.'

'Just go along with it,' she said. 'You've taken my brother's place, so you have to be him while you're here if you don't want tricky questions.'

'Yes, but what's ironing got to do with this weekend?'

She looked surprised at this. 'It has everything to do with it.'

It was on the tip of my tongue to ask her to explain that, but then I thought that maybe it wasn't only her parents who were out of their minds. Maybe out of your mind was normal here.

I went to the bathroom, squeezed toothpaste onto a finger, swiped my teeth with it, spat, rinsed, went to the bedroom that wasn't mine, got into the pyjamas that weren't mine either, and the bed (ditto) for my second night in the room that should have been Dawn Overton's. But I couldn't get to sleep. Kept thinking that along the landing was the little sister I didn't have. That downstairs were someone else's parents who thought I was their son. From there I got to thinking about Mum. My real mum. Who was going to the hospital on Monday about something so bad she and Dad wouldn't tell me. And I couldn't even be with her over the weekend, when she might need me.

Don't tell anyone or I'll set Stallone the dog on you, but I think I cried myself to sleep.

Chapter Eighteen

Saturday morning. Early. So early I didn't want to think about it, certainly didn't want to be awake in it, and wouldn't have been if Swoozie hadn't set her alarm to make sure I got up. I rolled out of my borrowed bed in my borrowed pyjamas, softened the gummy earballs, and popped them in place behind the McCue lugs. When I went down for some of the junk they called breakfast in that household I noticed the ironing board leaning against the wall by the front door and felt quite envious. I wanted to lean against a wall myself, but I had to go out there and Survive the Weekend.

Swoozie's dad had also got up early. He'd made me a packed lunch.

'What's in it?' I asked. 'Lettuce?'

'And celery.'

'Really pushed the boat out, didn't you.'

'There's also a vegetable pasty and some sesame seed crackers, some goats' cheese and a natural raspberry yogurt.'

'Ooh, can't wait.'

'I've polished your EI boots,' he said.

'My Eee-eye boots?'

He pointed to a pair of shiny orange walking boots. The kind of boots I wouldn't even wear in the dark. The sooner I got off this planet the better.

As well as the lunch box, Dad 2 had packed a sports bag full of things he thought I'd need for the weekend. I looked inside. Everything was so *neat*! If my dad packs a bag he grabs everything with his eyes shut, crams it in, and calls for me to sit on it while he tries to close the zip.

'I've put your costume at the bottom,' Dad 2 said.

'Costume?'

'Wrapped in tissue paper to protect it.' The doorbell rang before I could ask for more info on this. 'Get that, will you, Jug?' he said.

I went out to the hall and opened the front door. Eejit stood on the step with a lunch box and a sports bag like the one that had been packed for me. There was also something strapped on his back.

I scowled at him. 'What time do you call this?'

'Six-fifteen.'

'Well, go home, come back in twenty minutes.'

'We have to do a detour to Angie's.'

'What for?'

'She needs help.'

'What with?'

'I don't know. Stuff. She phones, we go, that's the way it works.'

'What's that on your back?'

'What do you think it is?'

I turned him round for a better look. It was an ironing board.

'Why are you taking that?'

'Well, I'd look pretty silly going without it,' he said.

'Silly *without* it?' I said.

'Come on. It's ten minutes' to Angie's and we have a bus to catch afterwards.'

I shoved something vaguely foodish in my gob, paid the bathroom a farewell visit, came down again, and laced my shiny orange boots. Eejit was in the hall now, chatting with Dad 2 and Swoozie.

'Ready?' he said to me.

I grunted and he reached for the ironing board

that was leaning against the wall.

'I'll give you a hand,' said Swoozie.

Then the two of them began strapping the ironing board to my back while I stood with my arms hanging and my jaw going up and down silently. What was *this* all about?

'Now you two be careful,' said Dad 2.

'That's right,' Mum 2 agreed, joining us in her dressing gown, hair standing up like she'd had a fright. 'Be creative, but don't take silly risks. We'll be proud of you even if you don't bring the trophy home.'

The father-who-wasn't-mine put the unnaturally healthy lunch box in one of my hands and the ultra-neat sports bag in the other, and Eejit and I were about to go when Swoozie reached up, pulled my head down, and kissed me on the forehead.

'Don't worry,' she whispered in one of my gum-enhanced ears. 'It's only a sport.'

With the things in our hands and on our backs, Atkins and I shouldn't have tried to get through the gate at the same time, but we did, and we ended up going through sideways, chest to chest.

As we set off across the estate I asked him why we were wearing ironing boards.

'You don't know?' he said.

'Would I ask if I did?'

'But I thought you were doing the same weekend with your Mr Rice.'

'Why would we take ironing boards on a Survival Weekend?'

'Survival Weekend? I thought you were joking about that.'

'A Survival Weekend's no joke,' I said. 'You think I wouldn't rather be at home reading comics with my feet up the wall? What's this one of yours about if it's not to teach us how to survive it?'

'It's the Nationwide Extreme Ironing Challenge.'

'The what?'

'The Nationwide Extreme Ironing Challenge.'

'The *what*?'

'The Nationwide Extreme Ironing Challenge. Teams from schools all over the country are gathering to compete for the trophy this weekend.'

'It's an *ironing* trophy?' I gasped in disbelief.

'I thought you knew.'

'Well I didn't. And we'll be ironing out of doors?'

'Yes. Before quite a big audience, I expect.'

'Ironing in front of a horde of absolute strangers?'

'And the judges.'

'Our ironing's going to be *judged*?'

'And marked accordingly. But the quality of the ironing will only be a part of it. It's *how* we iron that'll win us the big points.'

'How many ways are there to iron clothes?' I asked.

He frowned. 'We obviously should have gone over this with you.'

'That would've been nice,' I said.

So that's what last night's ironing practice had been about: to prepare me for what I had to do this weekend. Something came back to me that Mr Rice had said – thinking I was Juggy – as I was leaving Mr Numnuts' science lesson.

'I'm counting on you most of all. Whether we bring that trophy home or not could be your call.'

I supposed that meant that Juggy was pretty nifty with the iron. But he wasn't there. I was going to be taking his place. And I'd only held an iron twice in my life.

Angie lived on Richard Branson Crescent, where the houses had pillars and solid wooden doors instead of no pillars and white plastic doors.

'Which is hers?' I asked.

'The one with the lion on the gatepost.'

I growled at the lion as we pushed the gate back and hunched up the path with our ironing boards, lunch boxes and sports bags. I didn't feel right going to a house like this, but Eejit didn't seem bothered. He climbed the step and rang the bell while I climbed the step and stood listening to it echoing through the en-suites. When the door eventually cranked back I expected to see a butler on the welcome mat. It wasn't a butler. It was Angie's dad, Bill, who I hadn't seen since I was eight. He looked the same as I remembered only a bit fatter, with a moustache and a flashy gold medallion round his neck.*

'Hi, you two.'

'Angie asked us to come over,' Eejit told him. 'Said she needs help with something.'

---

* Only the medallion was round his neck. The moustache filled the gap between his top lip and his nose.

'She's got you well trained,' Bill said, widening the door.

We went into the hall. The house was much bigger inside than the ones on our patch. Probably because it was also bigger on the outside.

'Angie, your slaves are here!' her dad yelled up the stairs.

A distant reply from somewhere above. 'Tell 'em to wait!'

'You get that?' he said to us. Eejit said that we had, and Bill strolled down the tiled hallway to wherever it was he'd been before he came to answer the door.

I stared about me. What was an Angie Mint doing in a house like this? It didn't seem right. Not that I envied her, you understand. My house was as good as this – my real house, I mean, not Mrs Overton's. As good but a bit smaller, that's all, with fewer fancy touches and no chandeliers. All right, so some of our cupboard doors fell off occasionally, and our lights flickered every time a bike went by, and the downstairs toilet leaked, and there were cracks down a couple of the walls, and we had a burglar for a neighbour,

209

but apart from that it was as good as this.

'Hi, Juggy, hi, Ralph,' said Angie's mum, coming down the stairs in a black silk kimono with dragons all over it.

'Hi, Aud,' I said.

This seemed to surprise her, but she smiled anyway and went the same way Bill had, to the kitchen, I guessed. I get on great with the Audrey Mint of my world, but maybe this Audrey and Juggy weren't as close because they didn't see one another all the time. She might not be best buds with his mum either. Maybe this was the way things would have worked out at home if Bill and Audrey had stayed together. If my world's Bill had made money and he and Angie's mum hadn't split, they might also have moved to a house on Richard Branson Crescent.

When Angie came down she looked like she was going to a fancy hotel for the weekend instead of a couple of days' open-air ironing. I told her this.

'One must look one's best,' she said.

'Must one?' I said.

'Of course. If one doesn't, one might as

well stay at home.'

'One wishes one could.' I turned to Eejit. 'Is she always like this on her own turf?'

'Oh, no,' he said. 'Sometimes she puts on airs and graces. What do you want help with?' he asked Angie.

'I need a hand to pull my case.'

'Do we look like we've got spare hands?' I said, raising my two full ones and nodding at Eejit's pair of also full ones.

'What case?' said Eejit.

Angie pointed at something by the door. One of those folding trolleys with handles that Really Golden Oldies wheel their shopping home on. Except this one didn't have shopping on it. It had an expensive-looking suitcase.

'You're not taking that,' Eejit said.

'I need a few things,' Angie replied.

'Well so do we, but we're only taking what we can manage ourselves.'

'That's because you're not girls.'

'Why can't you pull it?' I asked her.

'Because I've done my nails,' she said, like this should be obvious even to a flat-eared knucklehead like me.

She flounced off and Eejit and I looked at one another.

'Isn't your Angie like that?' he asked.

'My Angie bites her nails. And if you try and help her with anything she thumps you.'

'Sounds like heaven.'

When she came back Angie was wearing white fur-topped boots, a matching hat, and a colour-coordinated cagoule.

'What's with the winter snow gear?' I said. 'It's not cold.'

'It might be later. We'll be out all night, remember.'

'We'll be undercover,' said Eejit.

'In tents. Tents don't have walls and central heating. Shall we go?'

She swept towards the door like a pop diva.

'Where's your ironing board?' I asked as she went.

She half turned and looked down her nose at me.

'What would I be doing with an ironing board?'

'You mean me and Atkins are ironing and you're not?'

'Atkins and I,' she corrected, and added loftily, 'I wouldn't soil my hands. Extreme Ironing's a *male* sport.'

She yelled 'Byeee!' to her parents, ordered us outside, closed the door, and started up the path with her polished nails standing out from her hips like flippers. Me and Eejit (Eejit and I) followed with our ironing boards, lunch boxes and overnight bags. As he was also pulling the suitcase trolley Eejit had a bit of a struggle. When he bounced the trolley off the fifth or sixth kerb on the way to school, Angie told him to watch out, which didn't help his mood all that much.

'If you don't like the way I'm pulling it, pull it yourself,' he snapped.

'All I'm saying is, be careful,' Her Royal Hoightyness said. 'There's some delicate stuff in there.'

'Like what?' he snarled. 'Frilly pink underwear?'

'No, *not* frilly pink underwear,' she retorted. 'I'm not a pink person.'

About a dozen kids were already hanging

around a green-and-yellow minibus in the car park when we got to Arnie Snit Compulsory. The driver sat behind the wheel cleaning out an ear and reading a magazine with the door shut, so no one could get in till he was ready.

'I hope this isn't the only bus,' I said.

'Why wouldn't it be?' said Angie.

'Well, you won't get two whole classes in that.'

'Two classes? It's only for the EI Team and the lottery winners.'

'Lottery winners?'

'There were just ten places for cheerers-on,' said Eejit. 'Those who wanted to come drew lots. Angie was one of the winners from our class.'

'How many are in the team?'

'Six.'

'Six? Just you, me and four others?'

'Hang on, let me count. Yes, four fingers and two thumbs make six.'

'And we're the only two from your class?'

I said this because there were three other ironing board wearers present and I didn't recognise any of them. One of them had a constant sniff that could really get to you if you stood near him for more than five seconds. 'That's Fuseli, Shenoy and Smee,' Eejit said when I asked who they were. 'We practice with them sometimes.'

'Here come the chiefs,' Angie said.

She meant Mr Rice and a woman I didn't know. They were carrying large sports bags with the word NASAL on the side. NASAL? Were they the bags they kept their lifetime supply of nose-drops in? More likely, it was this world's version of ADIDAS or NIKE, though for all I knew it could have been the initials of the National Association of Sweaty Armpitted Losers.

'Who's the one with the pudding?' I asked Eejit.

'Pudding?'

'Mr Rice.'

'That's Mrs Bevoir. She's here to look after the girls. Standing in for Miss Weeks while she gets over having Mr Rice's baby.'

'She's had a Rice baby as *well* as Miss Weeks?'

'No, I mean she's here in Miss Weeks's pl— '

I held my hand up to stop him. 'Kidding.'

Mrs Bevoir was dressed in normal clothes, but Mr Rice was in another of those romper suits he seemed to be so fond of in this world – a purple one today. As well as carrying his NASAL bag, he was pulling a trolley, quite a bit larger than Angie's, with a big box on top.

'Morning all!' he cried.

'Morning!' a handful of wide-awake voices cried back.

'Raring to go, team?' he asked those of us doing turtle impressions with ironing boards.

Atkins and the three I didn't know said, 'Yo, Coach!'

Rice noticed that I'd given the Yo a miss. 'Juggy?'

'What?'

'Raring to go?'

'Oh, I'm raring to go all right. Home.'

My usual Mr Rice would have barked at me for talking back that way, but this wasn't my usual Mr Rice. He came up to me, laid a giant mitt on my shoulder, and said, quietly, so no one else could hear, 'I know this is a nerve-wracking time for you, Jug, but if we don't win we don't win, simple as that. Just give it your best shot, eh?' Then he inspected the faces waiting for the bus. 'Where's Eric?'

'Here!'

Heads turned. Another boy I didn't know was hurrying towards us, lunch box in one hand, sports bag in the other, ironing board on his back. The team was complete. The bus doors clunked open. Everyone started to get on board. Time to go and make a lollipop of myself while people booed.

Chapter Nineteen

Don't ask me where the bus took us. The wilds, is all I know. There were some hills and some woods and a river, all that country-type stuff that's so bad for you, about two hours' journey from the school. Three other buses were there before us and two more turned up soon after. They left when everyone had got off and unloaded their gear. None of the school parties seemed keen to mix with any of the others, though some of the teachers marched up to one another and shook hands and chatted a bit. I asked Eejit how many schools were taking part. He said six. Six teams of six then, all competing to see who could do the best ironing. My mind boggled. Never again would I mock tattooed airheads who kick balls into nets and become millionaires with surgically-enhanced wives.

'This is the final,' Eejit told me. 'It's quite something to make it this far. Hundreds of schools were eliminated along the way.'

'Has your school ever done this well before?'

'No, first time. If we win, the school shoots up the league tables and the Head gets on the list of nobodies queuing to buy a knighthood.'

'So out of all the kids from all the schools who tried for this, your pal Juggy's one of the thirty-six best ironers in the country?'

'Yes. And it's iron-*ists*, not iron-*ers*.'

'And I'm expected to take his place. I, who have only used an iron twice in my life.'

'Twice? Come on. Don't you take turns with your dad at home?'

'Take turns?'

'With the ironing.'

I smirked. 'My dad doesn't know one end of an iron from the other, and I didn't myself till last Wednesday.'

'Who does the ironing where you come from then?' This was Angie, who'd just torn herself away from a heavy girlie chat about nail polish.

'The women, who else?'

'The *women*?' She reeled. 'Whoever heard of women ironing?'

'Except when they live alone and there's no man around,' Eejit put in.

'Except then. What sort of mad world do you *live* in, Jiggy McCue?'

'I used to wonder that myself,' I said. 'Not any more!'

'Well, all I hope,' said Eejit, 'is that on the two occasions you did the ironing you did a good job. I can stand not winning, but I'd hate us to come last after getting this far.'

'Take my advice,' I said. 'Get used to the coming last scenario.'

'You might be able to avoid that if the team puts on some really imaginative displays,' said Angie.

'What's imagination got to do with ironing?' I asked her.

She glanced at Eejit. 'He doesn't know?' He raised his hands helplessly. 'Looks like you should have dreamt up some routines for him,' she said.

He nodded gloomily. 'Yeah. A whole year of planning, training, additional weekend EI courses, all for nothing.'

'Come on, people,' said Mr Rice, jogging by. 'Get the tents up.' He jogged on to say the same thing to the other members of our team and support group.

There were five Snit Compulsory tents, three biggish ones and two single-person ones. The single-person tents were for Mr Rice and Mrs Bevoir, two of the bigger ones were for the supporters (boys in one, girls in the other) and the third was for the team. The other schools had similar arrangements and soon there were tents everywhere, in six groups. Everyone had to put their own tents up, even the teachers, or at least help in some way, even if it only meant holding a pole or moving the gear to make room for a groundsheet. My job turned out to be securing the guy-ropes.

'Why do I have to do the guy-ropes?' I asked Eejit.

'Because you're the guy-rope wizard,' he said.

'Me? I've never even tripped over a guy-rope.'

'You might not have, but Juggy has. There's a school camping trip most terms.'

'Holy macaroni.' School camping trips: one of my many visions of Hell. I looked at the ropes. 'How do you work these things?'

'You tie them to the ground pegs,' he said, a bit

sharply I thought, and left me to it.

I couldn't ask advice from anyone else – no one else in our team had even spoken to me yet – so I did the best I could and hoped it was OK for the ropes to be tied in bows.

'Why d'you think they're called guy-ropes?' I asked Eejit when he strolled back my way.

'What else would they be called?'

'Well, they could be called cricket bats, table mats or digital cameras, but I mean why "guy" ropes? If they have to be male why not man-ropes? Or boy-ropes? Or bloke-ropes, mate-ropes, even geezer-ropes?'

'You have a very weird mind, you know that?' Atkins said, and left me again.

When the tents were up, the teachers from the six schools emptied their NASAL bags. They all had them. Some also had big boxes like Mr Rice's, and they emptied these too. The bags and boxes contained the equipment the teams planned to use over the weekend. They laid all the stuff out for the judges to check that it complied with EIO* rules. I saw underwater goggles, crash helmets, coils of rope, lengths of chain, planks of wood, drills,

---

* The Extreme Ironing Organisation, which was running the show.

screwdrivers, and quite a bit more. One school had brought a couple of pushbikes, another a surfboard.

'As I'm sure you're aware,' the chief judge said when the equipment had been inspected and the teams were lined up for the Big Welcome Speech, 'any of the approved items may be used or adapted as aids to your displays. Natural objects found in the vicinity may also be used. In all heats but the first and last, two or more team-members may participate. The irons and heat pellets will be supplied by the EIO. You may use more than one iron at a time if you require it.'

'Heat pellets?' I said to Eejit.

He didn't answer. He was listening to the BW Speech.

'In the interests of safety,' the chief judge went on, 'I am required to stress that— ' He broke off when an ambulance pulled in where the buses had been. 'Perfect timing,' he said as a couple of medics got out. 'I was about to remind the contestants that in tournaments such as this, accidents can happen. Do not, whatever you do, teams, sacrifice care for the sake of effect. We do *not* want a repetition of last year.'

'What happened last year?' I asked Eejit.

'One boy broke an arm, another landed on his head and spent three months in hospital wondering who he was, a third went over a cliff.'

'Over a cliff? Was he hurt?'

'Dunno, our school wasn't in competition, but from what I heard the last anyone saw of him was his heels.'

'Now it only remains for me to wish you all the very best of luck,' the chief judge said. 'But remember, only one team can win The Golden Iron!'

'That's the trophy,' Eejit said.

'An iron made of gold?'

'Gold's the colour, doesn't matter what it's made of, it's such an honour to win it. The winning school keeps it until next year's tournament.'

I shook my head. This was sooooo sad.

'Mr Trumpkin, the irons, if you please!' the chief judge cried.

A very short Golden Oldie in a blazer threw back the lid of an old wooden box the CJ was standing behind. Everyone craned forward to see what was inside – a stack of old-fashioned irons, the non-electric kind, like the one my mother uses for a doorstop. A cheer went up like they were something special.

Finally the chief judge told us that there would be six rounds of six heats (six was obviously the magic number round here), three today, three tomorrow, and that the first would commence at mid-day, so we had two hours to check out the terrain.

'Look for ways of using our surroundings,' Eejit explained. 'Making the most of the environment is a big part of the challenge.'

'Team – to me!' (Mr Rice.)

The six members of our team, including me, went to him as ordered.

'Are you all right to go first with your speciality turn, Hot Stuff?' he asked one of the boys I didn't know.

'Sure am, Coach,' the boy answered with a cocky grin.

'*Hot Stuff?*' I rasped in Eejit's ear. 'Did he call him *Hot Stuff?*'

'That's his ironist name,' he whispered back.

'We all have one.'

Mr R told us to be back by half-eleven, in time to change for the first heat. What we had to do now, he said, was explore and make notes. Eejit said that I'd better go with him. We were just leaving when I heard Mr Rice say 'De-Wrinkle Man', which I ignored, but when he said it again, louder, Eejit tapped my arm.

'Coach wants you.'

'He does?'

'He called your name.'

'I didn't hear.'

'De-Wrinkle Man. Your ironist name.'

'De-Wrinkle Man? That's me? De-Wrinkle Man is the best anyone could come up with?'

'It's the name Juggy came up with.'

I was amazed. 'Why would he choose a name like De-Wrinkle Man? Why would *anybody*?'

'It's not easy finding a name that has something to do with ironing,' Eejit said. 'So many have been taken, and no ironist is allowed the same name as another.'

'I just wanted to see if you're all right,' Mr Rice said to me when we turned to him. 'You seem a mite distracted today.'

'Distracted,' I said. 'Yeah, that covers it pretty well.'

Eejit stepped in. 'He's having trouble deciding on the best manoeuvre for his solo tomorrow.'

'Well, whatever you do decide,' Rice said, again to me, 'make sure all safety aspects are covered,' and he added, with a chuckle, 'We want to be able to find *your* body, don't we?'

I flipped to Eejit. 'When you say "solo"…'

He grinned at Mr Rice. 'He's kidding. He knows that as our most daring and creative ironist he'll be doing the final heat tomorrow' – he glanced at me – '*alone.*'

'A-a-alone?' I stammered.

'Alone is how solos work,' said Atkins.

'Tell me,' I said in a surprisingly high-pitched voice. 'Are we anywhere near the cliff that kid from last year went over?'

Mr Rice guffawed at that. I was hilarious without even trying today.

While members of the six teams strolled in twos and threes around the local rocks, holes, water and cow dung, Atkins led the way past some straggly old woods. To take my mind off the news that I was our team's star turn, I asked him what his ironist name was.

'Iron King,' he said.

'Iron King? You're Iron King and I'm De-Wrinkle Man?'

'Yep.'

'Whaddayasay we swap?'

'I say go iron your ears.'

He had a notebook with him, which he kept stopping to write or sketch something in. I asked him what. He said he was looking for places that might be good for an ironing display, and that when we met up with the rest of the team we'd pool info and work out some strategies for the four multiple-ironist entries.

'Strategies?'

'We have to demonstrate the most unusual ways we can think of to iron things,' he said. 'The idea is to show how adventurous ironing can be in the natural environment.'

'The natural environment for ironing is inside a building,' I said.

'That's domestic ironing, not the extreme sport

variety. EI is about taking the activity as far as you can. Points are awarded for originality. The more unusual the display, the more points you stand to get.' He showed me some of his sketches. 'I'm making notes in words and pictures of trees and rock formations and anything else that might provide something to hang from, climb inside, that sort of thing.'

'Hang from? Climb inside?'

'Like the bough of this tree. See how it sticks out across the ravine? A competitor could be roped to his ironing board and hold on to the branch with one hand while pressing a shirt with the other.'

'That's insane.'

He grinned. 'Insanity's the name of the game.'

'What's the drawing of the nose all about?'

'That's not a nose, it's a pair of caves. I only drew them because…' He saw what I meant. 'Hey.' He went back a few paces and looked up at the hill we'd just passed. 'I didn't notice when I was drawing it.'

About two-thirds of the way up, there was a big rocky bump almost exactly like a colossal broken nose. The hill sort of leaned out at that point so the tip of the 'nose' hung over nothing. The two caves Eejit had drawn were underneath the bump, which made them look like its nostrils. He laughed when he saw this. I didn't. I didn't see *anything* funny in being here today.

When we'd done all the exploring and note-taking we could in the time, we headed back. When we met the rest of our team we squatted with them and swapped ideas. Well, they swapped and Eejit swapped, I kept my gap shut. I didn't get how these people could be so serious about ironing out of doors in the maddest ways possible. But serious they were, all five of them, discussing what stunts might gain the most points. Unbelievable.

'No thoughts from you, De-Wrinkle Man?' one of them asked.

He said it kind of sarcastically, I thought. The other strangers also looked my way like they weren't going to trade high-fives with me any time soon. The one with the snuffle – Smee – gave an especially noisy sniff as he looked at me, like it was me who'd given him that cold.

'Thoughts?' I said. 'Oh, you wouldn't believe the thoughts I'm getting.'

I was saved from sharing my true thoughts by Mr Rice, who bounced up and asked how it was going. He was behind me when he asked this, so I didn't see him at first, but when the others started telling him what they had in mind for the events he came round and squatted with us. When he did this, my eyes almost ignited. He'd changed out of the purple romper suit into a one-piece, neck-to-ankle, sky-blue costume with a yellow stripe down one leg. This might have been hard to take if it had been a loose garment, but it wasn't a loose garment, it was so tight that nothing, like *nothing*, inside it was hidden. You could see the outline of every rib, vein, nipple and wart, plus one or two other bits I definitely didn't want outlined for me. A squawk like a hen being strangled came from nearby.

'What was that, De-Wrinkle Man?' Mr Rice asked.

'Nothing. Just squawking.'

To keep my eyes from dropping below Rice waist-level, I forced them to stare without blinking at the little shield with the letters EIO on his skin-tight blue chest. When Atkins and I were alone again I asked him why our coach was dressed like that.

'How else would he be dressed?'

'How else?' I said. 'Well, jeans and shirt, say, or even the Teletubby romper suit, seeing as this is slap-me-senseless land. Anything but what he's got on now.'

'All the coaches dress like that,' Eejit said. 'Look around you.'

I looked around me. Saw three of the other male teachers in outfits just like Mr Rice's except they were different colours.

'We'd better get changed too,' Eejit said.

'Into what?'

'Our suits.'

I felt something in my throat. I think it was a tank. But I followed him to the tent. The other four team-members were already there, inside it, pouring themselves into a quartet of blue costumes with yellow leg stripes. I was still gulping like a goldfish down to its last gill when the Fantastic Four left – scowling at me, for some reason – until I realised something. I gasped with relief.

'I haven't got a suit like theirs!'

'Course you have,' said Atkins.

I grinned happily. 'I don't think I have.'

He dropped to his knees and unzipped the overnight bag Juggy's dad had packed for me. He rummaged, found what he was looking for at the very bottom, unwrapped the tissue paper, and held up a sky-blue one-piece that could only fit a five-year-old.

I laughed. 'I won't be able to get into that.'

He handed it to me anyway. 'Sure you will.'

I held the dinky little suit against my chest. Its ankles just reached my waist. 'I would if I was a doll,' I smirked.

'It's the same as mine,' Eejit said, pulling his shirt off. 'Same as the rest of the team's – and Mr Rice's. One size fits all. They stretch.'

My feet started to move.

'What are you doing?' Atkins asked.

'I'm jigging. It's what I do when I'm agitated.'

'If you say so.' He dropped his jeans. 'Come on, we're a bit behind.'

'We'll be all behind in these things,' I said.

He dropped his underpants and before I could

cover my eyes reached for the teensy little blue outfit he'd taken out of his bag. He shot a foot through a leghole, shoved his other foot in the other leghole, and pulled upward. The material stretched, just like he said it would.

'Aren't you going to wear anything underneath?'

'We're not allowed,' he replied. 'You can lose points for VPL.'

'VPL?'

'Visible Pant Line.'

He hauled the super-stretchy one-piece up his top half and jammed his arms in. I watched with a mixture of amazement and dismay as the material flattened across his chest and shoulders like it had been ironed there.

'Now you,' said Eejit Atkins, my Extreme Ironing team-mate.

Chapter Twenty

When I'd squeezed the totally starkers McCue bod into the super-stretch costume I looked down at myself in horror. How could one person have so many bulges in unmissable places? I'd worn the odd pair of huggy underpants in my time, but never a skin-tight neck-to-ankle one-piece – and underpants at least have the decency to hide under something else.

'I might as well be nude!' I cried.

'If you were nude you wouldn't be blue,' said Atkins.

'I would if I was cold.'

'With a yellow stripe down your leg?'

'I might have had an accident in a high wind.'

When we left the tent it was just me that was holding one hand over his hind-quarters and the other over his front.*

'You can't walk around like that,' Eejit said. 'People will stare.'

---

* When I say 'his' I mean my hind-quarters, my front, not Eejit's.

'You mean they won't if I don't?'

'Look at the others. Are people staring at them?'

I glanced at the thirty-four other team-members and the six coaches, all standing around in costumes as skin-tight as ours.

'Yes,' I said.

'Only because they're the centre of attraction,' said Eejit.

'Oh, they're that all right. You can see everything they've got, back, front and sideways. Why else do you think those girls over there are giggling behind their hands?'

'They're just happy to be here.'

'Good to know someone is.'

When we joined the rest of our team and Mr Rice, I dived into the midst of them so the spectators would get an eyeful of them rather than me. I didn't really listen to what Mr R and the boys were whispering (and sniffing in Smee's case) but I think it was something to do with what Hot Stuff was going to do in the first round. When the chief judge blew a whistle the teams had to go and stand in six separate lines, hands behind backs, feet spread, which believe me is not the way to stand if you're wearing a costume like that and don't want to be noticed. When I saw Angie waving from the mob of cheerers-on I did not wave back.

To decide the order the teams would go in, the six contestants who'd prepared for the first round's solo displays dipped into the pocket of an official shirt on a coat-hanger and took out a button. Each button had a number on it: one, two, three, four, five or six. Hot Stuff got the number four button. A bearded man in an Extreme Ironing Organisation T-shirt and track bottoms (lucky devil!) handed one of the official irons to the boy who'd picked the number one button. Just before he handed it over he slotted a heat pellet into the iron's base. The pellets kept their heat for about twenty minutes, Eejit said. Just long enough for each heat, you might say. Then, to encouraging wolf-whistles from his supporters, the first contestant – whose costume was emerald green with a red zigzag down the back – stepped forward with his ironing board.

'Ironing boards must be used in the opening heat,' Eejit whispered. 'After this we can iron on anything we like.'

'What else would you iron on?'

'Anything at all. Though ironing boards are used most of the time.'

Although the boy in green used his ironing board he didn't put it up. He placed it flat on the ground with its legs folded under it, threw his own legs up in the air, and, balancing on one hand, pressed a T-shirt with the iron in the other. There wasn't a sound while he did this. Silence was expected, Eejit said, so he wouldn't lose his concentration. When he'd finished he jumped right-way-up and his supporters shouted and whistled and stamped their feet while everyone else clapped politely. When an adjudicator examined the pressed T-shirt (only one side had to be ironed) he held up a card with a number 5 on it.

'Five out of ten for standard of ironing coupled with delivery,' Eejit said. 'Not bad, not great.'

Contestant number two was a thin blond kid with streaks in his hair from a school called Slitheen, Snivelling, Slytherin or something. His costume colour was black – handy, because it stopped the light picking out every nook and cranny of his body. Like the first contestant he left his ironing board on the ground instead of putting it up. When he was standing over it, a team-mate put a blindfold on him and the Extreme Ironing Org man gave him his heated iron. Then he spread his feet, tested his balance, bent over backwards, and started ironing a pair of boxer shorts like he always ironed upside down. When he was done he flipped upright, whipped his blindfold off, and saw that he'd missed a bit of the shorts – 'Not a good idea, the blindfold,' Eejit said – and, like the first contestant, was given five points. His supporters still applauded and stomped like crazy, though.

I won't describe what every contestant did, but our boy, Hot Stuff, pressed an apron as he roller-skated past his board, jerked himself around, and pressed more of it on the way back. He made four passes, ironing a bit more each time. He was awarded six points, which at the end of the heat put us neck-and-neck with the fifth contestant, who'd requested an extra iron so he could press a short-sleeved shirt on his grounded board with an iron on each foot and his arms folded.

As I hadn't gone out of my way to include myself in our team's chat about who was going to do what in which heat, the stuff they did in the second and third rounds that afternoon was as much of a surprise to me as what the other teams did. Some of the stunts looked quite dangerous while some were just plain nutty. The ironists had names like Crease Wizard, Steamer, Shirt Stuff, The Human Press, Laundry Basket, and The Scorcher. Here are some of the things that were done by various contestants and teams in the second and third rounds that day.

Ironing on a board held up by a team-mate lying on the ground.

Ironing in a hammock between trees, board across lap.

Hanging over the edge of a table to press something with an iron fixed to the top of the contestant's head.

Ironing while running between two team-mates on bikes, an ironing board stretched between them.

Ironing board suspended between the branches of a tree, contestant reaching down to iron from a higher branch.

Ironing the shirt on a friend's back while he lay face down in a stream breathing through a straw.

When the points were totted up at the end of the afternoon, our team was in third place. The lead team was from a school called Telmar Senior and the team a few points ahead of us was Lantenwaist Court. Mr Rice seemed pretty chuffed about our position.

'This is just Day One,' he said, rubbing his hands, 'and already we're third out of six. We're in with a chance, lads!'

'They're a bit strict on ironing quality,' said a boy who went by the name of Smooth Dude.

Mr Rice agreed. 'Those of you who'll be ironing tomorrow must pay special attention to the standard of your crease-work.' He turned to me. 'I hope your ironing's up to scratch, De-Wrinkle Man. If we're lucky enough to make it to second place in the fifth round your closing solo could be the decider. All our eyes and hopes will be on you with the spectacular finale you've been keeping so quiet about.'

'Spectacular finale?' I said faintly.

He laughed. He thought I was pretending. The others seemed to think that too, though they weren't laughing. Only Iron King Atkins knew that I had absolutely no idea what I was going to do tomorrow – or that I had almost zero ironing skills.

Chapter Twenty-one

That evening everyone except the EIO judges
(who'd shot off in taxis to a luxury hotel the
moment the day's heats were over) gathered round
a big bonfire well away from the tents. No luxuries
for us. Sleeping bags, hard ground, and food burnt
in the flames by the teachers. All this was bad
enough, but then a couple of brain-lites with a
guitar started singing *Old MacDonald Had a Farm*
and quite a few others joined in. They seemed to
have chosen this song because of the chorus line:
'Eee-eye-eee-eye-oh' – EIO, Extreme Ironing
Organisation, geddit? They followed this with *One
Man Went to Mow*, except their version was *One
Man Went to Iron* (a T-shirt, some Y-fronts, a
tablecloth, etc). By the time they started on *He'll be
Coming Round the Mountain with an Iron*, I was
sitting with my head covered, wishing I was on the
Ranting Lane Survival Weekend. No jolly sing-
songs round camp-fires there, bet your life.

The supporters were allowed to mingle with the teams now the day's events were over, so Angie joined Eejit and me in the firelight. The teams and coaches were back in civvies, which was a relief for me if no one else, after a day's walking round with my hand over my front bits.

'This is unreal,' I said.

'What is?' Angie asked.

'Whatever the turkey in this burger is made of.'

'It's Quorn,' she said when I opened it to show her.

'Corn?'

'Quorn.'

I slammed the bun shut. 'In other words it's made of nothing faintly resembling poultry.'

'It's vegetarian.'

'The bun might be, but I'm not.'

To tell you the truth, I was pretty fed up. I was the only one of our team who'd not been asked to help out in the second or third heat of the afternoon, so I'd done nothing but stand around trying not to bulge in my blue prat suit. I'd never been so bored.*

'What's the plan for tomorrow?' Angie asked

---

* Apart from every single day at school. Or when doing homework. Or shopping with my mum.

Eejit while I nibbled round the edge of the bun to avoid the fake turkey.

'You know we can't discuss team plans with outsiders,' he replied.

'I'm not an outsider, I'm a friend, a school-mate and a supporter.'

'An outsider is anyone who's not in the team.'

'Whisper to me,' she said.

'No. Wait and see.'

She turned to me. 'You'll tell me what's lined up for tomorrow, won't you?'

'I would if I could,' I said. The fact was, I hadn't paid much attention when the team talked about what they were going to do in the fourth and fifth rounds. 'Hey, it's getting a bit windy.'

'You mean you're not going to tell me either.'

'No, I mean it's getting a bit windy.'

It was too. And soon it was more than a bit. Inside of a minute the light breeze that ruffled hair became a gale trying to rip it out of our skulls. The fire flared like a huge pair of bellows had been rammed up it, pots and pans clanked without human hands attached, and there was a sort of billowing sound in the far darkness, like an enormous bird winging it for the hills. Then it started to rain. There were just a few little drops at first, but they were followed almost immediately by bigger drops that felt like they were seriously thinking of forming a society and becoming a downpour.

'To the tents!' a teacher bawled.

Oh dear, and I hadn't finished my phoney turkey burger.

Everyone jumped up and scrambled in different directions. Angie went to the girls' tent while Eejit and I headed for ours, which was one of the furthest from the fire and the terrific food. The rest of our team got there ahead of us, but they hadn't dived inside the tent like you might expect. They were standing in the wind and rain staring at the sports bags and ironing boards that weren't out in the open last time they looked.

'Where's the tent?'

'Are we sure this is where it was?'

'Course. That's our gear.'

'Anyway, look, the pegs are still in the ground.'

'It must have been carried off by the wind.'

'Must've. The guy-ropes can't have been secure enough.'

Everyone looked at me.

'Don't look at me,' I said.

'Who else would we look at?' one kid said. 'You tied them.'

If there'd been a high horse within arm's reach I'd have climbed up on it and galloped away, but there wasn't, so I went for indignant.

'Yes, I did,' I said. 'And who's the best guy-roper in this team? Juggy McCue, that's who. No, there was nothing wrong with those ropes,' I added, stooping to examine a rope-free tent peg. 'My guess is sabotage.'

All eyes popped. 'Sabotage?'

I raised an ultra-serious, solved-it eyebrow. 'What else could it be?'

'But who'd sabotage a tent?'

'This is a competition,' I explained. 'There are five other groups of people who might want to put the best of the opposition off their stroke.'

'But why us? We're not in the lead.'

Something flew at me on the wind and splatted round my face. I tore it off. 'Not yet we're not. But we could be by the end of tomorrow. Someone could have realised that.'

I looked at the thing in my hand. It wasn't easy to make out details in the darkness and wetness and windness, but it looked kind of furry, which is how it felt too. I realised what it was when Mr Rice ran up in his purple romper suit, snatched it off me, and jammed it on his head.

He was bald! Mr Rice wore a toupee!*

'I don't know what happened here,' he said, straightening his rug, 'but we must get you lads under cover before you get soaked and catch a chill. Let's go to my tent while we think what to do. Bring your gear!'

So we grabbed our bags and ironing boards and ran after him to his tent and stuffed ourselves and our things inside. As it was a one-person tent and that one was Mr Rice it was quite a tight fit – the half dozen ironing boards didn't help – and there was a honk of rain on steaming bodies that would have been a perfect target for one of my mother's so-called fresh-air sprays. While we steamed and cuddled our ironing boards, the rain hammered the canvas and the wind thumped it, and what-to-do-next type chat got started.

---

* It suddenly made sense that my own Mr Rice was one of those who exposed his skull to public gaze on Sponsored Baldness for Charity Day a while back (see *Ryan's Brain*). I don't know how he made it look like it was growing back afterwards, though. Must have speckled the bristles in with a felt pen or something until they looked thick enough to slam the horse blanket on again.

'We can't stay here, that's for sure,' said Smooth Dude.

Everyone mumbled amen to that.

'De-Wrinkle Man and I saw a couple of caves earlier,' said Atkins.

'Caves?' Mr Rice said.

'Up on the hill out there.'

'Are they accessible?'

'Think so. Bit of a climb, that's all.'

'We can't spend the night in a cave,' said Smee, the one with the drive-you-bonkers sniff.

'Anyone got a better idea?' Mr Rice asked. I suggested phoning for taxies to run us to the luxury hotel the judges had stashed themselves in for the night, but our secretly bald coach wouldn't have it. 'The ethos of these competitions is that they take place *away* from comfortable amenities,' he said.

'Wonder what sadist thought that up?' I muttered.

'We'll give the rain a minute to ease off,' Mr Rice said. 'Then check out those caves.'

We gave the rain a minute. Then we gave it five more.

'How's it looking?' Mr R said to Eejit, who was nearest the flaps.

Eejit peeked out. 'Like it's never going to stop.'

'Well then, we'd better make a dash for it. Agreed?'

Five people agreed. I wasn't one of them.

'Are you coming too, Coach?' Starch Fiend asked.

'Of course. I can't let my team spend the night alone in a cave, can I?'

I pointed out that if he went his tent would be empty.

'Yes,' he said. 'And?'

'Well, if you're not using it, one of us could.'

He looked around. 'De-Wrinkle Man's right. One of you could stay here...' But he said it like he'd be disappointed if anyone stuck a hand up and cried 'Me! Me!', so I didn't. When no one else did either, he said, 'I'd better tell Mrs Bevoir what's happening,' and we all leaned back so he could crawl over us and break our legs on his way out.

When he came back a couple of minutes later his rented hair was running into his eyes. 'Leave your boards but bring your overnight bags,' he commanded.

We left the tent hugging our bags to our chests or balancing them on our heads. It was raining as hard as ever and twice as windy. Perfect weather for six extreme ironists and their coach to jog up a hill in the dark. There was a path up the hill, which helped, and every so often we came across a skinny little tree to shelter under for a second or two, but we were still pretty drowned and windswept when we finally trotted into the nearest of the two caves Eejit and I had seen from the ground that morning. At first it looked like a very shallow cave, but as our eyes got used to the dark we saw that it went back a bit. If there'd been a light switch we might have gone further in, but there wasn't, and the only torch was the tiny one Mr Rice took out of a pocket in his Teletubby suit.

'Could be worse,' he said, pencilling the mini-beam around the rocky walls and ceiling.

'Could also be a modern house with central heating and fridge magnets,' I said.

Our bags contained all the usual overnight stuff, but Mr Rice had an extra item in his. He showed it to us in the narrow beam of the torch. 'My practice iron,' he said. 'As the judges are so strict on quality, those of you who'll be ironing tomorrow might want to get some last minute smoothing in.'

'I'll be OK,' sniffed Smee, wiping his nose on his sleeve.

'So will I,' said one of the others – Fuseli, I think.

'De-Wrinkle Man?' said Mr Rice.

'What?'

'Even if you've worked out a fantastic routine for your solo you could still lose vital points if your ironing's not perfect.'

He held up the iron, expecting me to take it.

'I'll think about it,' I said, shoving my wet hands in my windy pockets.

The truth was I had no plans to think about it. Not even one. The wally I was going to make of myself tomorrow was not terrifically high on my agenda of things to think about during a stormy night in a cave with a skinhead Mr Rice and five boys who thought of ironing as a sport and sang songs about it round camp-fires.

Chapter Twenty-two

The rain had stopped and the wind had died, and everyone but me was snoozing. I'd unrolled my sleeping bag near the back of the cave, a bit away from the others, and lay inside it with my hands under my head looking towards the cave mouth, which was chocka with stars. I swear I never saw so many stars. Some other time, another place, I might have really appreciated them, but now that it was so quiet all I could think about was tomorrow, when I was going to have to make an exhibition of myself in a figure-hugging suit before the wide eyes of strangers. Worse still, I was supposed to be the team's star ironist, but worse even than that was that I hadn't the faintest idea what I would do in my solo spot when my turn came.

I could just make out Mr Rice's practice iron from there. It stood where he'd left it, rimmed by starlight, like it was inviting me to pick it up. Maybe I ought to get some practice in after all. Maybe while I was ironing I would get an idea for my solo that wouldn't show me up too much. I wouldn't win the kind of points everyone expected me to, but I could always say the rubbish food had given me guts-ache or something.

I jemmied myself out of my sleeping bag and started forward. The stars were bright enough for me to pick my way between the other bags without tripping. I reached the practice iron. Mr Rice, snorting nearby like an old steam train, had left his little torch out too, and a heat pellet in case anyone changed their mind. I put the pellet and the torch in my pyjama pocket and was about to carry the iron off when I remembered that I needed some clothes to use it on. Mr Rice had slung some of his over a big stone. They'll do, I thought. He wouldn't miss them because as soon as I'd pressed them I'd return them. I bundled his togs under my arm and crept back to my sleeping bag, and past it, into the depths of the cave.

It was pitch black there and the torchlight didn't reach very far, but I found a boulder with an almost flat top and stretched one of Mr Rice's things out on it – a T-shirt with the words 'Extreme Ironing Coach' across the chest. I pressed the heat button on the pellet, the way I'd seen others do it, and slotted it into the base of the iron. Thirty seconds later the iron was hot. I stuck the torch in a rocky hollow so I could see what I was doing, and got to work. I pressed the T-shirt very carefully, and when I'd finished I swapped it for the top half of Mr Rice's romper suit. The material of this was thicker than the T-shirt and it kept ruffling up under the iron, so I had to go even more carefully with it.

While I was working, my mind wandered to the first time I'd held an iron, in the kitchen of The Dorks three nights ago, under my mum's command, and I felt myself get kind of misty-eyed. Then I remembered the medical condition of hers she was going to the hospital about on Monday, and my mind kicked up its spurs and galloped into worst-case scenario territory. Even worse than the worse-case scenario was that I wasn't there with her, and maybe never would be again. Maybe, if I ever did get back, it would be too late, and there'd be just me, Dad and Stallone (the cat version).

I shook myself. Stop thinking like that! Stop thinking anything but what to do tomorrow. I tried that, but nothing came. I pressed on.

The last piece of clothing was Mr Rice's skin-tight one-piece. It was much smaller without him inside it, of course, but not as small as the ones Eejit and I had put on. If it was true that all the suits started out the same size, Rice's bigger body must have permanently added extra centimetres to his in every direction. I laid the thing across the boulder and got stuck in. The seconds tiptoed by, until—

'Jiggy?'

I whirled round with the iron behind my back, so whoever it was wouldn't see what I was doing.

'Who's there?'

He came closer. 'Me. Eejit. What are you up to?'

'I thought that if I got some practice in, some ideas might come for my solo tomorrow.'

'Anything so far?'

'Not a stuffed dicky-bird.'

'Maybe we could work something out between us.'

'I could do with some input.'

I flipped the little suit over and started on the back. Eejit watched by torchlight.

'You sure do need the practice,' he said almost immediately.

'Oh, I thought I was doing quite a good job.'

'Not by competition standards. If the others saw the quality of your ironing, they'd tell Mr Rice that we might as well go home tonight.'

'If he agreed I'd be first in line.'

'They'd probably vote to leave you behind.'

'The others don't seem to like me much,' I said.

'They're jealous.'

'Jealous? Of me?'

'Of Juggy. Him being Mr Rice's star ironist and all. They think they're just as good. Looks like you're going to prove them right. More than right. Poor old Jug. If he ever returns, his reputation will be shot to pieces.'

'If this is an attempt to boost my confidence,' I said, 'maybe you should try harder.'

'Hey, what's that?'

'What's what?'

He whipped the torch from the hollow in the rock and trailed the light over the cave behind us.

'Woh,' he said.

I told him to keep his voice down and asked him

what he'd seen. He didn't answer, but went further into the cave, taking the light with him.

'Come and look at this,' he whispered when he was a dim outline against the rock.

I put the iron down and went after him. He was running the light over something long and thin that hung from the ceiling.

'Ever see one of these before?' he asked.

'Course. In pictures. It's a stalacmite.'

'If it was sticking up from the floor it would probably be a stalagmite,' he said. 'That's "g" as in ground. From the ceiling, like this one, it would usually be a stalactite − "c" for ceiling. Everyone knows that.'

'Stalactite,' I said. 'That's what I meant.'

'Only this isn't a stalactite.' He poked the thing with the end of the torch. 'A stalactite would be hard. This is quite soft.'

'So what is it?'

'A snottite.'

'A wottite?'

'A snottite. Look closely. What does it remind you of?'

I looked closely. It reminded me of a long

thick strand of nose-juice.

'Is it really called a snottite,' I said, 'or did you make it up?'

'It's really called that. I don't know much about them, but I think I read somewhere that snottites are bacteria that just grow and grow in the right conditions. I didn't know they grew in this country, so I've learnt some... Oh, look!'

The torch had picked out more snottites further on. He went to examine them. I followed. The deeper we went the more there were and the longer and thicker they got. Some reached all the way from the roof of the cave to the ground.

'There are dozens of them,' Eejit said excitedly. 'If this cave is really deep there could be *hundreds*.'

He went on. Seeing as he had the light, I went on too. We passed a spider hanging by a thread from one of the snottites, but Eejit was more interested in the snottites themselves than what lived on them. The cave was like a tunnel, but not a straight one, so we had to keep ducking and stooping and turning this way and that, always avoiding the snottites.

'How far are we going?' I asked.

'I want to see how deep the cave is,' Eejit said.

'It might go on forever.'

'Just a bit further.'

That bit further made the difference. The snottites started to thin out and the darkness got a little less dark. Then we saw stars.

'Another cave entrance!' Atkins said. He went ahead of me to the mouth of the cave. 'And guess which one. The other nostril.'

'Nostril?'

'You were the one who pointed it out. The way the hill bulged around the two caves like a broken nose?'

'Oh, yeah.'

I went and stood beside him. Far below were the tents that didn't include ours and the dull embers of the rained-on fire.

'We could take the short cut back,' Eejit suggested, meaning the narrow ridge that ran along the hill between the two caves.

'We could if we wanted to risk falling to pulp while screaming,' I said.

'OK. Back the long way, through the snott…'

He broke off.

'What?' I said.

'The spider we saw dangling from the snottite back there has given me an idea for your solo heat.'

'Oh yes?' I already didn't like the sound of this.

'From the ground these caves look like nostrils under a huge nose,' Eejit said. 'Well, imagine swinging from one of them like that spider.'

'Imagine swinging from a cave on a spider's thread?' I cried in horror.

'Not a thread, a rope. We dangle your ironing board from one cave-nostril and dangle you from the other. You swing across to the board and press an item of clothing while everyone down below shades their eyes to stare up in wonder. It'll be fantastic! A real show-stopper!'

'Heart-stopper, more like. Mine.'

'Those extra points'll be in the bag!' he said excitedly.

'Yes, and me along with them, zipped up on a stretcher. You're out of your mind, Atkins. Forget it.'

'I thought you said you wanted input.' He sounded kind of offended.

'I did. I do. What I don't want is to do spider impressions while hanging from a giant nostril in the sky.'

I snatched the torch off him and charged to the back of the cave and beyond, ducking and weaving round all the snottites. Eejit rode my heels, not wanting to be left alone in the dark, yammering his crazy idea all the way. Drawing near to our cave, I smelt something.

'Oh, no.'

I remembered that when I'd put the hot iron down to go and look at the first of the snottites Atkins had discovered, I'd intended to go back to it – and hadn't. I rushed to the boulder and seized the iron. The heat pellet was cooling now, but too late, the damage was done. I'd set it down on Mr Rice's all-in-one coaching outfit, and…

I stuck the torch between my teeth and held up the little suit. There was an iron-shaped hole in its posterior. A hole that would stretch and stretch when Mr Rice put the suit on. A hole that covered (or uncovered) the very place where he would slot his bare rump in the morning.

Chapter Twenty-three

It dawned. The Sunday I was to make a public prat of myself. It started a bit nippy, which I wasn't sorry about because when Mr Rice emerged from the depths of the cave in the costume he'd changed into in the dark, he also wore the top half of his romper suit, which covered the gaping burn in the backside.

'Let's hope it stays cold all day,' I whispered to Eejit. 'Are my ears straight?'

He reached behind my left ear and reshaped the piece of gum I'd stuck there.

The heats started earlier that day. The fourth round kicked off at ten, the fifth was due to start two hours later, and the final round, the solo heats, was set for 2pm. The judges looked like being even more strict than yesterday, telling us that if a team took too long to get started it would be eliminated from that round and the next team would be asked to step up.*

Eejit told me that because it was day two the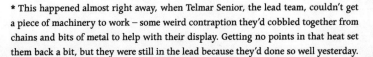

---

* This happened almost right away, when Telmar Senior, the lead team, couldn't get a piece of machinery to work – some weird contraption they'd cobbled together from chains and bits of metal to help with their display. Getting no points in that heat set them back a bit, but they were still in the lead because they'd done so well yesterday.

teams would be putting on more ambitious displays in the hope of earning more points – bad news for someone who hadn't thought of anything even slightly ambitious. Nothing at all, in fact. As time grew short and the ideas failed to pop into my head, I realised I had no choice but to go for Atkins's mad scheme. He was thrilled when I told him, but said we had to put it to Mr Rice. He also said we should make it sound like it was my idea, so we did. When he heard, the coach's features cracked into the kind of grin you'd expect to see on a lunatic who's just downed his second bottle of rum in ten minutes.

'I love it! I knew you had something up that blue sleeve of yours, De-Wrinkle Man!'

The coaches weren't allowed to help their teams during a heat, only advise them, and Mr Rice's advice was to take whatever equipment we needed up to the caves and get everything ready well in advance. The only equipment we needed were two long lengths of rope, one shorter length and my ironing board. The two of us carried them up to the first cave, where Atkins outlined a ten-point plan he'd devised to make the most of my display. While he told me the plan I leant against a rock wishing he was the other Eejit, who never had a bright idea in his miserable little life. Here are the ten points.

1: In Cave One, tie the two long ropes round the ironing board, one at each end to balance it.

2: Peg an item of clothing to the ironing board.

3: In Cave Two, tie the shorter rope round an ankle of the solo contestant (me).

4: Just before the start of the display, lower the ironing board out of Cave One so that it hangs in space.

5: When the starter whistle goes, lower the contestant out of Cave Two by his ankle. When he and the ironing board are level they will look to the spectators below like they're hanging on snot-strings from a big nose.

6: The contestant swings to the ironing board and holds on to it.

7: The contestant does some serious upside-down ironing for about thirty seconds.

8: The contestant swings away from the ironing board and is hauled up into Cave Two.

9: The ironing board is carefully lowered to the ground for the judges to inspect the quality of the ironing.

10: Wild cheers break out and the contestant (in a coma) wins a massive amount of points.

Because there was still quite a bit of time before it was my turn to hit the fan, we went back down for the sandwiches that were on offer. Veggie sandwiches. 'You know, this is an obsession,' I said, peering at the wad of foliage inside my two planks of granary. But I bit into it because it might be the last thing I ever tasted.

Today, there was something new in the middle of the central space where most of the ironing displays took place: an ironing board that didn't belong to any of the teams. Its legs had been painted black, a piece of red cloth was draped over it, and sitting on the cloth was the trophy we were competing for. The Golden Iron was pretty much like the competition irons, just a bit bigger, and of course gold-coloured. Team-members and coaches kept going up to it and touching it for luck. I didn't bother. Luck had never worked for me before, so why would it change its rotten ways now that I was going to come flying out of a giant hooter in the sky with a rope round my ankle?

Because the day was slow to warm up, almost all the team-members and coaches wore something extra over their top halves till the second round of heats. Eejit thought this was because the judges were wearing coats and didn't like to ask us to strip when they had no plans to. He was probably right, because when they eventually took their coats off they ordered us to lose ours too. The only people puzzled by the crowd-wide gasp and the titters as the sun smacked Mr Rice's bare kazoo were those who were facing the other way. These were the judges, Mrs Bevoir and Mr Rice himself. Eejit and I walked smartly from the scene, urgently inspecting our fingernails and whistling unknown tunes.

We managed to keep out of Mr Rice's way after that until just before the final round, when he came across us down the far end of the central display area.

'What a result!' he crowed. 'The superb efforts of Starch Fiend and Smooth Dude have put us in second place, just five points behind Telmar!'

'It helped that Lantenwaist Court made such a mess of ironing under that waterfall,' Eejit reminded him.

'It helped, but without our boys' efforts we still wouldn't be this close to taking the Golden Iron home.'

'That's not gonna happen,' I muttered.

'Now I don't want to hear that kind of talk,' he said, still smiling. 'You'll do a grand job, Juggy, I know you will.'

'I'll do a grand job of breaking my neck or some other part I'm quite attached to,' I said. 'I have no experience of hanging upside down from high places by an ankle.'*

'Well, I'll be happy if you keep us in second place,' Mr Rice said. 'To come second in a

---

* This wasn't quite true. Not so long before, I'd hung out of a high window in nothing but a musical jock-strap while my father held my ankles. I still shudder when I think of that, but if you must hear all the embarrassing details you can tick them off one by one in a tale of woe called *Neville the Devil*.

tournament as prestigious as this is a heck of an achievement. Look, even the press have turned out for it.' He waved at a bunch of reporters and photographers, who waved back. 'They must think our team's got something. They keep snapping me. Asking me to do press-ups, knee-bends, flex my muscles with my back to them. They're not asking anyone else to do things like that.'

'Bummer,' said Eejit.

Mr Rice glanced at him. 'Sorry?'

'Bare-faced cheek. Taking so many pictures of you.'

'Mm, yes, s'pose so.'

'Have you arsed them?'

'Asked them?'

'Why you and no one else?'

'Well, not in so many words, no.'

'Maybe they got wind of what a great coach you are.'

'Oh, surely not.' But he blushed as he said it.

'Any flashing? Of their cameras.'

'Not that I noticed. The sun's quite bright now.'

'Well, try not to crack, sir.'

'Crack?'

'Under the strain of all the exposure. We need you behind us.' Eejit shivered suddenly. 'Still a bit breezy down the bottom here, isn't it?'

'I was thinking the same thing myself,' said Mr Rice. 'I'd better be getting back. Good luck, De-Wrinkle Man. Knock 'em dead up there!'

'Sooner them than me,' I said.

He headed back to the men from the press, his cargo hold bobbing cheekily in the sunshine. The photographers grinned at one another and hoisted their cameras. They were having a peach of a time.

Some of the displays in the first two rounds of the day had been quite clever and some had been seriously bananas. Most had taken place in the central space, but some of the more imaginative ones hadn't, so the crowd was constantly moving to see them. Here are some of the ones I saw.

A contestant folded over the bough of a tree ironing a hanky on a fellow team-member's head. Six points.

A contestant with an ironing board on a surfboard (on the river), ironing an apron. Awarded just one point because he toppled in and his apron drowned.

A contestant ironing on top of a human pyramid formed by his team-mates. Eight points.

Synchronised ironing with dance steps by four team-members to *Hit Me Baby One More Time*. Seven points.

Ironing on a board while windsurfing. The wind fell. So did the contestant. Two points.

A giant catapult made from tree branches and heavy-duty elastic. Contestant fired at ironing board, broke his nose when he smashed into it but awarded three points for effort.

Ironing while doing the splits, irons on both feet, two ironing boards set quite a way apart. Contestant almost lost his gooseberries on a passing hedgehog but gained seven points.

The six contestants for the final round stood to get double points if their solos really impressed the judges. And wouldn't you know it, when we took our order buttons from the Official Shirt pocket I got number six, which meant I was going last. My nerves were already in rags, and now I had to wait to the very end to get it over with. Angie popped out of the crowd to make me feel better.

'We're all counting on you, so you'd better be good,' she said. Like everyone else except Atkins and Mr Rice, she had no idea what I was going to do.

'Get ready to be disappointed,' I scowled.

'If you were Juggy,' she said, 'I'd give you a good-luck hug.'

'Just as well I'm not then. Musketeers don't do hugs.'

'You're not a Musketeer now, you're one of The Four.'

'I'm starting a rule book for us. Zero hugs are Rule One.'

She went back to the crowd.

I didn't watch any of the other heats in that round. Didn't want to know what the competition did. If they were really good, I would look even more pathetic that I expected to. I went up to Cave One and sat chewing my nails alone. Eejit joined me about 2:45 with the iron and heat pellet he'd collected from the organisers. He also brought another kid from our team to help out – Smee, the one that hadn't stopped sniffing since we started out. His ironist name was Board Stiff, but Board Sniff would have suited him better. He wasn't just sniffing now either. He'd been sneezing since he woke up, and he had sneezes like no one else except my dad's, which are so sudden and table-rattling that it takes your heart ten minutes to settle down after each one. Getting soaked in last night's rain had brought his cold to a head, he said.

'Just keep your lousy germs to yourself,' I said to him. 'It's going to be bad enough hanging over nothing by a rope without sneezing what's left of my brains out.'

But then I had a thought. I switched on the famous McCue charm.

'Tell you what, you're about my height. No one'll notice all the way down there at the centre of the earth if you take my place. How about it? The glory will be all yours.'

'If I take your place,' Board Stiff sniffed, 'everyone'll think I'm you from a distance, which means you'll get the glory, not me, so thanks hugely for the offer but bog off.'

'Tie that end, will you?' Atkins said to him.

The two of them got to work fixing the pair of

long ropes round the ends of the ironing board while I stood in the cave's gloom and my own, thinking that this was it. My time had almost come.

'Instead of just standing there,' Eejit said, 'why don't you go next door and take some deep breaths before jumping head-first to your death?'

I gulped.

'Joking,' he said with the kind of chirpy little laugh that makes you want to smash faces in with mallets.

'Where's the torch?' I growled.

'I forgot it.'

'You * it? You mean I've got to walk through all those snottites in total darkness?'

'Yeah. Mind your head.'

I started towards the back of the cave.

'Take the third rope,' he called. 'And the iron. And the heat pellet.'

I grabbed the rope, the iron and the heat pellet, barged into the deep darkness at the back of the cave, and banged my head on a snottite.

Chapter Twenty-four

When I got to the approximate snottite where we'd seen the spider that had put this whole stupid idea into Atkins's head I thought that here was one spider that deserved to have its thread snapped. The reason I didn't snap it was that I couldn't find it in the dark. Also, snapping the spider's thread might have tempted fate. Mine. In a few minutes I was going to be swinging on a thread of my own, with a looooong way to fall.

When I reached the second cave, I sat just back from the mouth and tied the rope in a triple knot round my left ankle. Then I leaned out, very cautiously. Way below, dozens of little blobs were watching the last-but-one solo heat. I could just make out what they were seeing. The competitor, standing on the parallel crossbars of two bikes with an ironing board fixed across them, was pressing a piece of material or clothing while somehow steering the bikes in figures-of-eight.

Clever. Could earn a bunch of points, enough to win maybe, but even if he messed up and fell off he wouldn't have far to drop. Unlike me. With all that empty space between me and the ground, I suddenly realised that I wasn't terrifically fond of heights. Well, no, heights are fine. What I'm not terrifically fond of is being up on them. Especially when the plan is for me to be thrown off them to iron something upside down in mid-air. My mother's hair would have immediately turned white if she'd known about this.

'Better tie the rope round your ankle,' Atkins said, emerging from the dark at the back of the cave.

'Already have.'

'Yes, well I seem to remember that you also tied some guy-ropes to some pegs and a breeze puffed the tent away, so I think I'd better check, don't you?'

With a flick of the wrist he undid the rope I'd triple-knotted so tightly and started again. When he'd finished, it felt like I'd need a blowtorch to get me out of it. He looped some of the loose rope round a pillar of rock at the back of the cave.

I asked if he was sure it would hold.

'Pretty much,' he said. 'With the two of us on the end you should be fairly safe if you don't wriggle about too much.'

'I won't move a millimetre,' I assured him.

He went to the mouth of the cave and looked down. 'They'll be ready for us in a minute.'

'Us? You're coming too then, are you?'

He laughed. Well he would, wouldn't he? He was going to be safe and sound up here while I was... I tried to blank my mind.

'I'll go and give Board Stiff a hand to lower the board,' Eejit said. 'We have to get it in place before you go out.'

'Don't forget to come back, will you?' I said.

'If I forgot to come back,' he said as he vanished into the snottite-filled darkness, 'there'd be no one to lower you out of the cave.'

'Correction!' I shouted. 'Forget to come back!'

I went once more to the cave mouth and looked over. If anything went wrong – like if the rope round my ankle snapped, say – five minutes from now I'd be Spam. I saw my ironing board being lowered from the neighbouring cave and Eejit and

Smee leaning out a little. When the board caught on a bit of rock they twitched the ropes to work it free. Then it was clear of the hill, turning a little this way, a little that, with nothing except a big bunch of air between it and the earth way below – just as I was going to be very, very soon.

In a minute I heard a loud sneeze echoing through the snottites behind me and Atkins and Board Stiff stumbled out of the darkness.

'Ready for the off?' Eejit asked me.

'No.'

He went to the edge and looked over.

'They seem to be ready for us down there. Better get in position. Once the whistle goes we'll have to lower you right away. If we're too slow starting we could be eliminated from the round, which, with the way the points are stacking up, means we could be back in third place, maybe even fourth.'

'I'm happy with fifth,' I said.

'Well, no one'll be happy with you,' he said. 'What you have to do...' – he put his mouth to one of my sticky-out ears so Smee wouldn't hear – '…is get out there and iron as only De-Wrinkle Man can, and make the school proud of him.'

'Why would I care if the school's proud of him?' I whispered back.

'You don't have to care. Just remember who's holding the rope.'

'You wouldn't.'

He twisted his mouth at me. 'Tempt me.'

I was staring at him, wondering what he might do if I let his team down, when Board Stiff sneezed so loudly we almost flattened our haircuts on the cave roof.

'You ought to take something for that,' I said, jamming my spine back where it belonged.

'I will,' he said. 'Right after your funeral.'

'Talking of which…' Eejit said.

It was time.

I got down on my knees like I was about to pray, inched to the edge of the cave mouth, and looked down through all the empty nothingness that ended with very solid somethingness. My audience was staring up at me, eagerly waiting to see what I would do.

And then the whistle went.

'Move out a bit further,' Eejit said behind me. 'It's OK, we've got the rope, you won't fall.'

'Could I have that in writing please?'

'Later,' said Smee. 'While they're scraping you off the ground.'

'Atkins,' I said, 'why did you choose that sniffy little ray of sunshine to help you?'

'He's the only little ray of sunshine who would,' he answered. 'The rest blame you for losing the tent.'

'So do I,' sniffed Smee. 'I just wanted to be in at the kill.'

The rope round my ankle jerked suddenly. My heart smacked me under the chin.

'*What did you do?*' I cried in italics.

'Just checking the tension,' said Atkins.

'You don't need to check it, just ask.'

'Go on, De-Wrinkle Man, over you go.'

And over I went. Slowly, slowly, the front part of my skin-tight pratsuit scraping rock as I slithered out and down, head first. I heard a sound nearby. 'OoooooOOOOOOOO,' it went. It was me.

Now I was completely out of the cave, upside down against the rock, going down bit by bit by bit, the rope squeezing the blood and bone out of my ankle.

'You're heavier than you look!' Eejit shouted from somewhere above me.

'Don't say that!' I yelled back.

'Don't worry, we've still got a grip – just! Say when you're level with the top of the ironing board! Can't see from in here!'

The board hung three or four metres away, from the other nostril.

'I'm level!' I shouted.

'Good! Now push yourself towards it!'

I bent my knee – the one that wasn't attached to the leg whose ankle had a rope round it – and shoved myself away from the hill. Not hard enough, though, because I went less than a metre before crashing back.

'What was that jerk?' Eejit shouted.

'It was me!' I replied.

'At last he admits it!' Smee said.

'Did you make it to the ironing board?!' Eejit asked.

'No! Gotta try again! Get ready for another jerk!'

'One's enough!' Smee again.

I prepared to kick harder at the hillside. If I got it right this time, I would swing across and grab hold of the ironing board and start to press the pair of boxer shorts Eejit had pinned to...

Oh no.

'Atkins!' I called.

'What?!'

'I've forgotten the iron!'

'What?!'

'You'll have to pass it down on another rope!'

'We hadn't got another rope, you twonk!'

'There's no need to be insulting!'

'There's *every* need to be insulting! How could you forget the iron?! Ironing's what this is all *about*!'

'You might not have noticed,' I shouted back, 'but I had a couple of other things on my mind when I left the cave!'

'Hey, look at this.'

Smee said this. Not to me, though I heard him. I wanted to know what was so interesting up there that they had to look at it rather than concentrate on keeping me from decorating the ground. 'Look at what?' I demanded, spinning slowly round while the blood rushed to my hair.

'The rope!' This time it was Atkins.

'What about the rope?'

'The one round your ankle's one of the long ones! It should be the short one!'

'What difference does the length make?'

'It makes ALL the difference! It means that in the dark we got them mixed up! It means that someone who wasn't me...'

'Don't blame me,' Board Stiff said.

'I do blame you!' Atkins yelled at him. 'I checked the rope I tied round my end of the ironing board!'

'I checked mine too, but it was dark.'

'And in the dark you used the *short* one!'

'Like I said' – this was me – 'what difference does it make if I've got one of the long ropes round my ankle instead of the short one?'

'It doesn't make any difference to you!' bawled Atkins. 'But it'll make a hell of a difference when it comes to lowering the board to the ground for the judges to check the quality of the ironing! It'll make that difference because one of the ropes it's hanging from ISN'T LONG ENOUGH TO GO THAT FAR!' He was getting quite worked up by the sound of it. 'What a disaster,' he wailed. 'My carefully-thought-out plan ruined by you two. McCue forgets his iron and one of the board's ropes is too short. And they call *me* Eejit!'

'I'm going to sneeze,' said Board Stiff.

'Well don't do it over me,' Eejit snapped.

'Uh… uh… uh…'

And then it came. The biggest, most cave-shaking, most echoey sneeze I ever heard while roped upside down in mid-air. Such an ear-shattering sneeze that the sneezer couldn't possibly have kept a grip on a rope he was holding.

And he didn't.

I knew the rope had lost one of its grippers when it went a little slack. When it went a lot slack I knew that Eejit hadn't been able to hold me on his own. As the rope started to unreel I headed earthward, and because dive-bombing through nothing isn't one of those things I do for pleasure my feet started jigging about. During one of the jigs I kicked the hill, which pushed me clear of it, into a big wide arc. As I swung across the arc, the rope got longer and longer, and when I reached the end of the arc I started back, in another arc, and when I reached the end of this one I started on yet another, and all the time I was getting nearer and nearer to the ground and closer and closer to the eyeballs staring up at me. I would like to say that I kept bravely quiet during this little adventure, but it wouldn't be true. Waving my arms and kicking wildly all the way, I bawled, at the top of my voice:

Mummmeeeeeeee!!!

I was vaguely aware of my audience leaning back from the central arena I was heading towards. I was just as vaguely aware of Mr Rice running forward: to my rescue? I never found out. I was two metres from the ground when I reached for something – anything – that might stop me swinging into the orbit of Mars. My hands closed on two things, though I didn't pause to check what they were. In one hand there was something hairy. In the other there was something that felt like a handle of some sort. The something hairy felt so weird that I let go of it immediately – it soared away from me and disappeared into the trees – but I held on to the handle thing. A handle couldn't stop me flying through the air, but handles are usually attached to something, and that was promising, even if the only thing it was attached to was me.

So, holding the handle, I swept upside down over the space where many of the ironing displays had been staged. Over it and back, and over it again, on the end of the long rope. I should have been even closer to the ground by now, and not swinging, but (I heard this later) the end of the rope up in the cave had caught on something, and held. If I'd known this I would have thrown an immediate party, with balloons and paper hats and cake, because it stopped me just in time from standing on my brain in a McCue-sized molehill. The handle I was holding was quite heavy, but it was all I had to hold on to, so I just let it hang at the end of my arm, but each time I reached the middle of the open space there was a jolt and a flash of red, like blood. I dreaded to think what the jolt and the red flash were all about. Had I killed something? Someone?

Chapter Twenty-five

It was Angie who told me how it had looked from the ground.

'We saw the ironing board hanging from the cave,' she said. 'Then we saw you dropping from the other cave on the end of a rope. (Hey, did you know those caves and that bit of hill look like a nose from below?) Then we saw you pretending to be too feeble to push yourself to the ironing board. Then you waved your hands to show that you hadn't actually got an iron. Then we heard this signal*, and next thing we knew you were falling and falling, and honestly, I thought you'd had it. But then you were swinging in these great sweeps like Tarzan in the jungle, but upside down, screaming like a madman as you grabbed Mr Rice's wig in one hand, the Golden Iron in the other. Then you tossed the wig into the trees and swung back to press the red cloth on the Iron's board — with the Golden Iron itself! Then you swung

---

* The almighty sneeze in the cave that had caused Board Stiff to let go of the rope and start my dive to the ground from the nose on the hill (you could call it my nose-dive).

forward again, then back again, and forward again, ironing more of the cloth each time, until you stopped swinging and the rope round your ankle loosened and you dropped into the inflatable paddling pool used by the last team but one. I tell you, McCue, I never saw anything so mad or brilliant. Nor had the judges, you could tell. For what you did, they could even forgive you using the trophy to iron its own cloth – great bit of ironing too! – and even for cracking its ironing board on the last swoop. Incredible!'

And then she hugged me, even though I was still dripping from the paddling pool. And I let her. It was the nearest I could get to a Mum-hug, which I badly needed after the most terrifying experience of my life, especially as I had to make out that what everyone had seen had been my carefully-planned ironing display.

You may not be surprised to hear that because of the way it looked from the ground I got such a load of points that I won the tournament for Arnold Snit Compulsory. Yes, me, yours truly, I, Jiggy McCue, with my 'extremely daring and skilful ironing display', as the judges put it when they handed our team the Golden Iron.

As we started for home, Eejit and Angie phoned their parents to tell them when to expect them back, and Angie told me to phone Juggy's parents with the same info. Once I'd done that I scrunched up in a corner of the bus and shut the world out. The part of the world I most wanted to shut out was the bit with Mr Rice in it. He sat at the back in Mrs Bevoir's bright yellow folding rain hat, not speaking to anyone, me most of all. He wasn't speaking to me for two reasons. The first was that I'd exposed his baldness to the whole wide world by throwing his wig into the trees, where a fierce bird had instantly made a nest of it and refused to let him have it back. The other reason was that right after the wig incident someone finally told him that he'd been flashing his raw tomato all afternoon, then someone from our team – not sure who – slipped him the word that he'd seen me sneaking into the back of the cave with his practice iron and costume the night before, which meant that it had to be me who'd caused him to hang out in public all afternoon. When Mr Rice realised why the photographers had been snapping him in all those macho poses, the blood drained from all four of his cheeks.

It was almost dark when the bus pulled in at the school. Parents were waiting for some of us, including Eejit's and Angie's and Juggy's dads. Miss Weeks was there too, with her baby strapped to her chest, and she'd brought a spare wig for Mr R, which he put on under cover of an umbrella. He smiled a bit once it was in place, but not at me. Wouldn't come anywhere near me, even though I was the hero of the hour, the day, the weekend, the year.

Back at the house Janet and Dawn Overton should have been living in, there was a lot of typical Golden Oldie fussing – 'You must be starving, now tell us all about it, every last detail' – and when all that was out of the way (I only told them what I thought they'd want to hear) the parental types went off and watched telly, leaving Juggy's little sister and me sitting at the kitchen table.

'Now how did it *really* go?' Swoozie asked.

I told her. The truth, not the official version. She rolled her eyes a few times, dropped in the odd question, said 'Holy ironing boards,' twice, and when we were done…

'We missed you.'

'Missed Juggy, you mean,' I said.

'Same thing.'

'Not quite.' I waggled my gum-enhanced ears at her.

'When are you going to try the broom cupboard again?' she asked.

'Tomorrow at school, if I can get in there.'

'What if it doesn't work again?'

'It's got to.'

'But what if it doesn't?'

We just looked at one another across the table. She was probably thinking the same as me. Like, if I didn't get back through the broom cupboard I could be stuck here forever, in the wrong house, with the wrong parents, at the wrong school. I would always have to wear chewing gum behind my ears, Pete Garrett would never be my friend again, and Swoozie would always have to pretend to be my sister. It didn't bear thinking about. Well, most of it. Maybe I could live with the last bit.

Next morning, as I was leaving for school, Swoozie slipped something into my jacket pocket when her parents weren't looking.

'What's that?' I asked.

'Some biscuits so you don't go hungry before lunch.'

It was such a nice thought that I didn't know what to say. Then she threw her arms round my waist and squeezed.

'And what's this for?'

She smiled up at me, a bit sadly I thought. 'It's for in case you make it through the broom cupboard and I never see you again.'

At school that morning we only had half a lesson before first break – Maths, no loss – because the Head had called a Special Assembly. When a Special Assembly's called at Ranting Lane it usually means we're going to be told off for something, or given bad news, or warned about some dodgy character hanging round the school gates. But this wasn't that kind of Special Assembly. As you know, the Head at Ranting Lane is Mr Hubbard, but the Mr Hubbard of Arnie Snit taught a potty religion about aliens, and the Head was an old geezer in a tweed jacket with leather elbows called Professor Kirke.* The Prof wanted to show the Golden Iron to the whole school and say a few words about our efforts over the weekend. He said the few words, then called me and the rest of the Extreme Ironing team onto the stage to shake our hands and give the Specially Assembled kids a chance to cheer us. It felt strange being cheered on stage. The only other time it ever happened to me was when I was in the Infants. I was playing a Heavily-Bearded Wise Man in a Christmas nativity play and I accidentally dropped my little sack of chocolate coins and jumped off the stage to get it back. That wasn't when they cheered, though. On the way back up the steps I fingernailed one of the gold wrappers off and shoved the coin in my infant trap. Then I screwed my face up and turned to the audience, and said 'This is wubbish,' which covered the play pretty well too. That's when they cheered.

After the Special Assembly and the cut-down Maths it was morning break, and time for another shot at getting home. Eejit and Angie went to the

* The *Head* was called Professor Kirke. The leather elbows were called Leather Elbows.

broom cupboard with me, but it wouldn't have mattered if I'd gone alone because the door was open and Mr Heathcliff was there, talking to Mrs Bevoir about dusters or something. All we could do was slide by and hang around the corner, looking round every minute or two to see if they'd gone yet.

While we were waiting I took out the biscuits Swoozie had dropped in my pocket. She'd put five chocolate digestives in a little plastic box that was just big enough for them. The box was pink and it had ponies all over it. Sweet. Eejit smirked until I told him that Swoozie had given it to me because she didn't want me to be hungry. Then he said he wished he had a sister, and I gave him one of the biscuits. I offered Angie one too but she said she was watching her figure.

I was just slotting the last choc dige into my gap when Angie said: 'I think they're going.'

She was right. Mr Heathcliff was locking the broom cupboard door and strolling away with Mrs Bevoir. I put the empty biscuit box back in my pocket and asked Eejit if he'd got his skeleton keys.

'Yes.'

'Remember which one fits?'

'Yes.'

'Come on then. This could be the time it happens.'

We pushed the door back – just as the bell went. I said something unprintable as all the really keen students ran to the doors and stampeded over us in their eagerness to get back to their lessons.

'This is never going to work,' I wailed as we picked ourselves up and went with the flow.

'Yes, fate doesn't seem to be on your side, does it?' said Atkins.

'Nor yours if you want the third Crapologist back,' I pointed out.

'*Cavaleiro!*' he snarled.

'Still, if that's the way it has to be,' Angie chipped in, 'we could do worse than be stuck with you.'

This was one of the few kind things she'd said to me in the three or four days we'd known one another. 'Thanks,' I said.

'Not a lot worse, though,' she added. 'You being such a whinger and defeatist with such a warped sense of humour and all. But I suppose you *could* be worse.'

The next lesson was English. I wouldn't have minded that if I wasn't so disappointed about not being at Ranting Lane.* The English teacher was Mrs Gamble, the same as at RL, and she smiled at me whenever I gave the right answers (every time) to her questions about grammar and punctuation, but looked kind of surprised too, so maybe Juggy wasn't the wiz at her subject that I was. Getting things right in English made me feel a bit better about being in the wrong world, and I got to thinking that maybe I could make a go of it there if I really had to. Eejit might become a proper friend in time, Angie too maybe, even though she was a bit more girly than I liked, and now that I was the Extreme Ironing king I was somebody for the first time ever. I kind of liked being somebody. Naturally, there would be a few problems if I had to stay. Like the food. If they thought I was going to eat leaves for the rest of my life they were thinking of the wrong bunny. But there were good things there too. Swoozie, for one. That little kid would be a definite bonus.

We were only about a third of the way into the

* And I never thought I'd say *that* in this lifetime!

lesson when Mrs Gamble decided to stop talking without notes and opened a paperback to read something to us. I thought I heard her say a word under her breath that teachers aren't supposed to say, specially old teachers with wrinkles, but then she looked up and told us that she'd forgotten her reading glasses.

'Don't worry about it, Miss,' said Wapshott. 'You just rest your ancient eyes and we'll go for early dinner.'

'Kind of you, Ian,' she said, 'but I'll try and soldier on. I must have left them in the science lab.' She said the last bit more to herself than us.

'What were you doing in the science lab, Miss?' Sami asked.

'Mr Numnuts is off sick today,' Mrs Gamble replied, 'and and other teachers are taking turns to mind his classes in his absence.'

'Know much about science, do you?' Marlene Bronson asked. Anything to throw a teacher off their stride, even teachers we like. It's the principle of the thing.

'Next to nothing,' Mrs G admitted. 'I did half a crossword while the students got on with some revision. Look, while I'm struggling to see this ridiculously small print I wonder if one of you would be so kind as to go to the science lab and look for my glasses?'

She peered round the suddenly blank faces before her, and finally slapped her orbs onto her best student.

'Juggy, would you go? They'll probably be on the desk.'

'What's it worth?' I enquired, the way you do.

'How about not getting a thick ear for cheeking a beloved teacher?'

'If McCue's ears got any thicker,' said Ryan, 'he'd never get out the door.'

'They helped me fly through the air and win the Golden Iron,' I said as I shunted to the front. 'Something you couldn't have done, dirt-box.'

'You'll have to fetch the key to the lab from the office,' Mrs Gamble said. 'I'll give you a note for Miss Prince.'

She scribbled something on a pad and tore the sheet out. I folded it into my top pocket and went out sideways like a popular actor leaving the stage. This fame thing is cool.

I collected the key from Miss Prince without any trouble, except a bit of misery-mouth – 'Bring it back the moment you're done there!' – and went to the science lab, where I found that I didn't need the key after all because the door was open. The head cleaning lady, Queenie Sidaj, was in there, dropping anything she didn't like the look of into a bin on wheels. I saw a glasses case on the desk, but didn't like to go in uninvited. I cleared my throat in the doorway. Mrs Sidaj glanced my way, saw that I wasn't a grown up, and scowled.

'You want something?'

'My teacher left her glasses here and sent me to fetch them.'

'Well *I* don't know where they are!' she snapped, like I'd accused her of nicking them.

'No, I think that's them on the— '

'Just don't disturb me while you look for them,' she said, hauling cupboard doors open and looking inside for things to feed to her wheelie. 'Some of us have work to do.'

'I won't say another word,' I said.

'What?'

'I said I won't say another word.'

'Make sure you don't. What's this?'

I would have said 'What's what?' if I hadn't just made two promises never to speak again. Queenie was wearing rubber gloves, but even with them on she didn't seem keen to handle what it was she took out of the cupboard. I went over. She'd found Mr Numnuts' two boxes of Turkish Delight with added flavouring. Because the boxes were transparent you could see the changes that had already started to occur inside. The pink cubes were redder now and the blue cubes were closer to purple. But it was the sugary coating that had changed most. On the pink cubes the sugar had started to crack, like they'd been left out in the sun too long. On the blue cubes it was going furry.

'It's one of Mr Numnuts' experiments,' I said, blowing the vow of silence in eleven-point-two seconds.

'Experiments!' she snorted, and dropped the two boxes in her bin.

I was so shocked by this that I forgot to be scared of her. 'But we wanted to see what happened to the cubes!' I cried.

'Did you now?' she growled. 'Well, I'll not have

rotting food in my school, so you'll have to see it somewhere else!'

She slammed the cupboard door and went to the next one, hauled another something out, chucked it in the bin, and was on her way to the one after that when the theme tune for *The Simpsons* started up. She tore a phone from a pocket of her dungarees, and began giving instructions to her old man, who from the sound of it was ringing from a supermarket. 'No, the chicken-flavoured ones, it was on the list, wasn't it? And you know what cheese to get, I've told you a thousand times. What do you mean you can't find any of the— '

I stopped listening because now that she'd turned away to have this private conversation about shopping I saw my chance to save some of the Turkish Delight to show Mr Numnuts and the class if I had to stay here till our next lesson with him. I couldn't take the boxes, because Queenie might rugby-tackle me if she saw bulges in my pockets that hadn't been there before, but I thought I might get away with a couple of sample cubes if I was quick – and I had just the thing to put them in. I bent over the bin, flipped the lids of Mr N's two boxes, and popped one pink cube and one blue cube into Swoozie's little pink pony box. I dropped the pony box back in my pocket, licked my fingers, and stepped away from the bin just as Queenie switched her husband off and turned round.

'Ah, there they are!' I said, scurrying to the desk and picking up Mrs Gamble's glasses case.

'You got what you came for then?' the Queen of Charm barked.

'Yes.'

'Well get outta here and let me get on with my work.'

I got outta there.

Chapter Twenty-six

I returned the unused key to Miss Prince, who was about as grateful that I'd been so quick as Queenie had been for my company, and started back to class. To get to Mrs Gamble's from the office you had to pass the gym. I walked past the gym the same way I'd passed it on the way to the office, with bent knees, so only the top half of my head would be seen if anyone inside glanced my way. Just enough height to chortle at the bunch of saps doing the pointless exercises that give the lesson its bad name. Better this side of the glass than theirs, I thought, until a voice shouted a name too much like my own for comfort, and the door sprang back and Mr Rice stood there. The very Mr Rice I'd managed to avoid all morning and wanted to carry on avoiding.

'Juggy,' he said again. 'A word.'

'Sorry, sir, can't stop,' I replied. 'Urgent mission for Mrs...' − No, don't tell him whose class I'm in, he might come for me there – '… for a teacher!'

I scuttled round the nearest corner, then the next, hoping he wasn't hoofing after me. But he was.

'Just a minute, Juggy, please!'

Panic. Hide. But where? There was only one door in sight. Was it unlocked? Was there anyone the other side of it? I turned the handle, opened the door – no light on, good sign – and plunged in. I closed the door, stepped backwards in the darkness, and bumped into something that made me sit down hard. The tumble made a bit of a clatter, so I sat absolutely still, fingers and toes crossed that Mr Rice hadn't heard and would fling the door back and find me sitting on… what? I felt below me. Something hard and cold, like a bucket. A bucket? Hey. Of course. I hadn't thought where I was going in my panic, but here I was in Mr Heathcliff's broom cupboard!

I was still realising this when light splurged briefly behind me and I heard a small click like a door closing. Hang on. The door was in front of me. The last thing before the back wall was the row of workcoats…

I heard something moving back there. I jumped to my feet.

'Hello? Anyone there?'

But it wasn't me who said this. It was someone else. Someone using my voice.

'Er…' (*This* was me.)

'Who are you?' the other voice whispered.

'Who are *you*?' I whispered back.

'It's not… Jiggy, is it?'

My heart bounced around my ribs for a while and came to rest in my throat. 'Juggy?' I said.

'At last!' he cried.

'At last?' Me again. 'What do you mean, at last? I've practically taken up residence in this crummy cupboard trying to get back.'

'*You* have!' he said. 'I've been in here every chance I got.'

'Oh. Really. Different times to me then, obviously.'

'Obviously.'

'Well now that we've finally made it at the same time,' I said, 'maybe we can get back where we belong.'

'Can't be soon enough for me,' he said. 'Did you

take my place like I took yours?'

'Had to, no choice. How did you get on?'

'I managed. Even if it was like going from a starring role in Hamlet to an outtake from Home and Away.'

'How were my friends?'

'Some friends. Garrett, of all people. Give me Eejit any day. My Eejit. Yours is a cretin.'

'Yeah, well your Angie's a bit girlie.'

'I like her that way. Yours might as well be a boy.'

'I like *her* that way. How'd you manage with the physical thing?'

'Physical thing?'

'The ear situation.'

'Double-sided tape. Extra-adhesive.'

'Who thought of that?'

'Angie. What did you do about yours?'

'Put wads of chewing gum behind them. Your sister's idea.'

'Not the chewing gum under my bed?'

'Yes, why?'

He groaned. 'I was building that gumball into a record-breaker!'

'Well you'll have to rebuild it, won't you? It took

some hefty lumps to stack my ears like yours. How do *sleep* with those things? Can you lie flat? Do you have to sit up all night?'

'Are you making fun of my ears?' he asked.

'Fun?' I said. 'Ears like that are no fun. I speak from experience.'

'How would you like it if I made fun of your jigginess?'

'You can't make fun of my jigginess. You haven't seen it at work.'

'Oh no? I got action replays wherever I went. People kept asking why I wasn't flapping my arms and dancing whenever the slightest thing went wrong. You wouldn't believe the number of impressions of you I had to put up with. Quite an act you have there.'

'It's not an act. It's me, I can't help it. If I didn't do all that stuff I wouldn't be Jiggy McCue.'

'Like if I didn't have these ears I wouldn't be *Juggy* McCue.'

Put like that we were about even.

'Why did you come in here in the first place?' I asked.

'What, just now?'

'Last Thursday.'

'Mr Lubelski was coming. I keep out of his way as much as possible.'

'Why? Mr Lubelski's one of the nicest teachers at Ranting Lane.'

'Lucky you. The one at ASC isn't nice – to me anyway. It's because I can't see the point of art. He shouts at me in Polish all the time.'

I'd never heard my Mr Lubelski even raise his voice, in any language, so this was a surprise, but hearing that my double wasn't into art surprised me even more. Art's one of my two best subjects.

'Why did you come in here?' Juggy asked.

'Last time or this time?'

'This time.'

'Mrs Gamble sent me to fetch her glasses from the science lab.'

'What was she doing in the science lab?'

'Minding Mr Numnuts' class. He's off sick.'

'Well, your Mrs G asked me to fetch her glasses too, but from the staff room. We'd better swap in case their eyesight's slightly different or the frames aren't the same.'

We groped for one another to exchange the

glasses. I shuddered when our hands touched. Think he did too. Touching yourself in another body is not a terrifically comfortable experience. When we'd made the switch, he asked me if I'd taken his place in the EI tournament. I said that I had.

'And?' He sounded kind of nervous about my answer.

'And I brought home the Golden Iron.'

I heard him gasp. 'You won the trophy?'

'Almost single-handed. Juggy McCue's the big cheese at Arnie Snit.'

'Whew. I was scared you'd ruin my rep.'

'Ruin it? I made you a hero. How was the Survival Weekend?'

'I didn't go.'

'You didn't go? But you had to. Everyone did whose parents sneakily signed the permission form when we weren't looking.'

'Made out I had a sore throat. You think I wanted to go on a two-day endurance course with my ears taped back? It's because I didn't go that I dodged in here just now. Mr Rice saw me from the gym and was coming after me, yelling. Probably wants to have a go at me for skipping his rotten weekend. Your Mr Rice is terrifying.'

'Oh, I can handle him.'

'You're welcome to him. Come on, let's do this. The Mrs Gs will be wondering where we've got to.'

'Fine by me. Just make sure you go past me and not back to Ranting Lane.'

'No problem. All I have to do is keep going forward. Make sure you do the same or there could be two of us at my school.'

'You know, this is pretty amazing, isn't it?' I said.

'What is?'

'All this, us, everything. This is a perfectly ordinary broom cupboard except when we're both in it at the same time, then it's got a door at each end, each one leading to an alternative version of the school.'

'I wonder if it's just us?' he said.

'Just us?'

'Well, suppose, say, your Eejit Atkins and my Eejit Atkins also went into their school broom cupboards at the same time. Would they switch?'

That made me smile. Alternative Atkins's might

be even harder to disguise than alternative McCues.

'Let's go,' said Juggy. 'Ooh, I can't wait to get back to proper food!'

'You call what you eat *proper* food?' I said.

'Thousand times better than the high-fat unhealthy garbage you like.'

'Thanks for your opinion. Watch how you go, there's a bucket h—'

Clang.

He'd kicked the bucket.

Clang.

He'd kicked it again, deliberately this time.

I pushed my way through the smelly old workcoats and felt for the back wall. I found it, except that it was no longer a wall.

'I'm at my door,' I said.

And, from beyond the coats: 'And me.'

'So. This is it.'

'Yes. None too soon either.'

I turned the door handle. 'Say goodbye to Swoozie for me. I'll miss her.'

He didn't answer. He was back in Arnold Snit Compulsory. And I—

'McCue! There you are! What the devil do you mean, running off when I call you?! And what are you doing in that cupboard?! Why aren't you in class?!'

I laughed. I couldn't help it. I closed the broom cupboard door for the last time. I was *never* going in there again.

'And what's so flaming funny?!' Mr Rice demanded, marching up to me in his stupid red tracksuit.

Chapter Twenty-seven

'Explain!' Mr Rice bawled, glaring down at me from the summit of Everest.

'Mrs Gamble asked me to get her specs from the staff room,' I said, pulling the glasses case from my pocket to prove it.

'Mr Heathcliff's broom cupboard is nowhere near the staff room!' he bellowed.

'I got lost.'

'Lost?! In a cupboard?! What kind of fool do you take me for, boy?!'

I put my fingers to my chin. 'You'll have to give me a minute on that one, sir.'

'And what's happened to your ears?!'

'Oops, forgot.' I took the gum from behind my lugs. 'I was trying something.'

'Trying something?! Trying what?!'

'To see if I could cruise in high winds.'

'Are you trying to take me for a ride, McCue?!'

'Would if I could, sir, but you need a licence for

hauling men in red.'

'Less of the lip! Why weren't you with us at the weekend!'

I remembered Juggy's excuse, made a phlegmy sound in the tonsil area, tried to speak huskily. 'Sore throat. Very bad. My mum kept me in from Friday night till this morning.'

'Do you really expect me to believe that?!'

'No, course not. You wouldn't be you if you believed me.'

'What's that in your pocket?!'

'My pocket? I showed you. Mrs Gamble's glasses.'

'The other one!'

I looked at my other jacket pocket. It bulged.

'Oh, that's nothing.'

He snorted. 'Nothing! I catch you in the caretaker's cupboard with a bulging pocket and you say it's *nothing*?! Show me!'

He held his enormous hand out, fingers twitching fiercely.

'It's just a little box,' I explained.

He wasn't having it. 'Let me see!'

I took Swoozie's biscuit box out. He scowled at it.

'That's *yours*?'

'It is now.'

'But it's… pink!'

'So?'

'Well, not very masculine, is it!'

'I know. I'm working on that.'

'Open it!'

'You don't really think I stole a little pink biscuit box from the school caretaker?' I said. 'What would Mr Heathcliff be doing with a box like this?'

'Open it!'

'You'll wake the school if you keep shouting like that,' I told him.*

'OPEN IT!' he screamed. 'AT ONCE!'

I opened the box. He bent over it to peer inside.

'Uh?!' he said intelligently.

'It's Turkish Delight,' I said.

'It's like no Turkish Delight I ever saw!'

'This is special. My mum has it sent from Turkey. You can't buy it here.'

He studied the two little cubes up close. 'This blue one, it's… furry!'

'That's the secret Turkish ingredient.'

'Looks like the beginnings of mould to me!' he boomed.

'It is mould,' I said. 'Didn't you know that real

---

* Oh, it was good to be back!

blue Turkish Delight always has mould? Edible mould, of course. Like you get on those stinky blue-veined cheeses.'

He looked up at me from his crouch over the box. 'You mean Stilton?! Gorgonzola?! Camembert?! I love those cheeses!'

'Well, you'd probably love this then.'

'Where can I get some?'

'Try Turkey. If you're quick, you could get a one-way flight today.'

His eyes flipped back to Swoozie's box. 'Does your mother have any to spare?! Just a sample, so I can see if I like it!'

'No. Sorry. This is the last.'

'Oh. Pity.'

He stood up straight, towered over me again, obviously disappointed that he couldn't get his jaws round some mouldy Turkish Delight.

'Tell you what,' I said. 'Why don't I give you this piece?'

'Eh?!'

'Yeah, why not? Go on, help yourself. Just the blue one, though.'

'But it's yours!'

He was so surprised that I would give him

something for free that he looked quite shaky for a sec. I switched on my most endearing smile (the one I melt my mother's heart with when she's in a lather with me).

'My way of saying sorry I couldn't make the weekend,' I said. 'I was so looking forward to it too.'

'You were?!' he said in disbelief.

'I should say. Learn to survive? Top of my list of things to do, survive.'

I offered the little box. He hesitated – still a bit suspicious, probably – but then picked up the mouldy blue cube and popped it in the Rice fodder gap. He started chewing immediately, and a second later pulled the kind of face people pull when they're thinking of spitting something out, and his neck started to glow, and the glow spread up to his cheeks, and his eyes went round like something out of this world had just reached his inner taste buds (which it had in a way). When he gulped the last of the cube down, his Adam's apple bobbed, and his lips spread across his face like a bad accident. When they reared back to make way for a grin, I saw that his teeth were blue. And furry.

'Now that's what I *call* Turkish Delight!' he said.

'All you need now is the flying rug,' I said, 'and you're off.'

One of his hands started towards his hair, but stopped half way. Was his secret out? Did everyone *know*?

'F-flying rug?' he stammered, for once not booming.

'I mean flying carpet,' I said. 'Turkish Delight, flying carpets, they kinda go together.'

'Oh! Yes! See what you mean! Ha-ha!'

And he swung round and jogged off like his feet were on springs. I watched him go, shaking my head in amazement. Who would have thought that peed-on Turkish Delight could have such an effect?

I was just approaching Mrs Gamble's room when the lunch bell went. People were jumping up from their desks and streaming towards the door as I streamed in.

'At last!' Mrs G said. 'I could have got them myself if I'd known you were going to be this long.'

'Sorry, miss. Got laywaid by Mr Rice.'

'Laywaid?'

'Waylaid. I kept telling him I had to get back, but I couldn't stop him banging on about sporty stuff.' I handed over her glasses. 'Did I miss much?'

She shook her grizzled old head. 'Nothing you can't catch up on.'

'OK. Bye, miss.' I went to the door. 'Good to see you again!'

She looked surprised at this, but I went out before she could ask what I meant.

Angie was waiting for me in the corridor. 'You want to have another go at the broom cupboard?'

'Are you kidding?' I said. 'I'm never going near that cupboard again.'

'What? After all you've been saying about wanting to get home?'

'No. Think I'll stay. I like it better here.'

'Since when?'

'Since now.'

'But you don't *belong* here!'

'Who's to know?'

'Well, I will for starters.'

'Yeah, but you won't tell.'

'I will! I want my Jiggy back!'

I felt my eyebrows lift. '*Your* Jiggy?'

'I mean the McCue that belongs to this school.'

'What do you want that loser back for?'

She scowled. 'Jiggy McCue might be a loser. He might be pain in the bum. He might make my life a misery because of the things that happen to him. But he's my friend. Our friend. Pete's and mine. You're not. I want you gone and him returned.'

It was hard to keep a straight face. 'You'll get used to me.'

'I won't,' she said. 'You'll never take Jig's place. Jiggy hates healthy food. His bedroom's a tip. He has a wonky way of looking at things. He cheeks the teachers. He gets detentions like you probably get badges for good behaviour. He's... unpredictable.'

'And these are *good* things?'

'No, but they're him.'

It sounded like this was as near to praise as I was going to get.

'Do me a favour, will you?' I said. 'The tape behind my ears feels loose. Will you check it for me?'

I turned round so she could look behind my ears. She cleared the hair away to get a good decko.

'Where is it?'

'Where's what?'

'The tape.'

'Can't you see it?'

'No.'

'Well, it should be there,' I said. 'If they were Juggy's ears.'

'Yes, but it's...not.'

There was a longish pause, during which I could almost hear the cogs of her brain passing one another. I smoothed down the hair behind my ears and turned round. Waited for her to realise.

'Jiggy?' she said, finally.

I spread my hands. 'The one and only.'

And she thumped me. Hard, on the shoulder. Then she gripped me by the armpit and frog-marched me to the lockers to collect our lunch boxes. I looked at mine with affection. Real food again!

'How long have you been back?' she asked as we went outside.

'Since just before the end of English.'

'You came from the broom cupboard?'

'Where else?'

'And Juggy?'

'We passed in the dark.'

'In the dark of the broom cupboard?'

'No, in the dark of the icecream parlour in the shopping arcade.'

She squinted at me. 'You haven't changed. Still a smart-arse.'

'It's my trademark. Wasn't he a smart-arse too?'

'Not so much, no.'

'I hear he managed to skip the Survival Weekend. You and Pete go?'

'Oh yes, we went.'

'Have a good time?'

'Good time? It was the most miserable weekend of my life so far.'

'That go for Pete too?'

'Pretty much. He's not talking to you, by the way.'

'Why, what have I done?'

'He didn't believe Juggy wasn't you.'

'How could he think he was me with those ears?'

'He thought you'd done something to make them stick out and got all uppity when the joke went on and on.'

'Some joke. Didn't you put him right?'

'Try and put Garrett right when he gets a fixed idea in his feeble brain? You know how far that gets you.'

We were almost at our private bench in the Concrete Garden when I spotted Atkins trading punches with a couple of pals. I went over to him.

'Hi, Eej, how's it hanging?'

He paused mid-punch. 'Whatcha, Jig. 'Ow's yerself?'

'Not so bad. Yer dad knocked over any good chemists lately?'

He jaw hit his kneecaps. 'Wot?'

I took him by the arm and walked him away from his thump-buddies.

'I know he's not a landscape gardener,' I whispered.

'Oo said he was?'

'That's what everyone things he is. Atkins, I know your secret.'

'Wot secret's 'at then?'

'That you're not really as stupid as you make out.'

'Er?'

'I've often thought that no one could be as thick as you *and* comb his hair.'

'I don't comb me 'air.'

'Figure of speech. Just wanted you to know that it won't go any further.'

'Wot won't?'

'Your secret.'

'Wot secret?'

I winked at him. 'OK, Eej. Got it. Between ourselves, eh?'

He went even blanker. When he puts his little mind to it, my version of Eejit Atkins can be blanker than an ungraffitied wall.

'Jig…' he said.

'Wot?'

'You ent 'alf bin pecoolia these last foo days.'

''Ave I?'

'Yer. But don' worry abaat it.'

He tapped a finger against the side of his nose. Then he skipped away to fump his mates some more.

Chapter Twenty-eight

Angie wasn't kidding about Pete not talking to me. He even swapped seats with other boys in a couple of classes so he wouldn't have to sit next to me. I could live with that. I was back, that was the main thing. Home ground, familiar territory, faces I knew on people I knew. You won't believe how comforting it is to know that the person you're talking to is the person he or she looks like. I was even pleased to see my teachers' features.

After school, Angie grabbed Pete and made him take a slow stroll round town with us while we tried to convince him about what had happened and that I hadn't been pulling his doodah. He still didn't seem too sure by the time we'd finished, but that was Pete all over. He never likes to back down or give in.

From town we headed for the real Brook Farm Estate. When we reached our street I gratefully watched P and A fighting on the step of the house across the road to try and be first inside, then went round the back of my house – number 23! I hauled myself up the gate, reached over, slipped the bolt, swung in, shot the bolt again, and started along the path. Round the fence corner I saw my kennel, and this time no lousy dog stuck its muzzle out to snarl at me. Better still, the good old garden gnome was beside the back step. I went to it, bent down, slipped the key out of its behind, and kissed it. The key, that is.

I unlocked the back door and was treating my senses to the genuine McCue atmosphere of the once and future house, when I saw Stallone slinking towards me, glaring at me with those mean green eyes of his. I dropped my bag – my own bag, which Juggy had left by my desk in English – fell to my knees, and reached for him.

'Come here, you mangy critter!'

Stallone snarled, reached for me in return, and scratched my hand. But I didn't mind. I was so happy to be home.

Without even bothering to take my jacket off and chuck it at the wall, or even dart into the kitchen to plug my face, I ran up to my room. My real room. My sanctuary. I threw the door back – and froze, staring. It was so tidy it looked like someone else's. But of course it *had* been someone else's. For four nights it had been the resting place of a neat freak. I went in. Opened my wardrobe. My shirts hung so perfectly they could have been in a window display. I opened my underwear drawer. It should have been all over the place because I spend so much time rooting around in there for pairs of pants I can stand being seen dead in. But today every pant and T-shirt was stacked in perfect alignment with all the others, and there wasn't a crease in one of them, except where there should be.

I looked around some more. My slippers stood to attention behind the door, toes facing the wall. My chair was placed just-so under my desk. The desk was shinier than it had been when Mum assembled it from the flat-pack. I spotted the Musketeer Rule Book. At least that wouldn't have been tampered with. I picked it up, read the stirring words 'One for all and all for lunch', flipped the cover to read the four rules I'd laboured so hard over, and found... a fifth rule! It was in my own handwriting, underlined just like the others.

Rule 5: Musketeers must keep their rooms tidy at all times!

I closed the book with a growl, wishing I'd thought to add a rule to the Three Carrotlovers Rule Book.

'Jiggy? That you up there?'

My mother, calling from downstairs. I hadn't heard her come in. Maybe she'd been in all the time, in the kitchen or living room. But what was she doing at home at this time of…?

I remembered. It was the day of the hospital appointment. The appointment I'd been dreading because I just knew there was going to be bad news. Probably the worst news imaginable.

'No, it's the burglar from next door,' I called.

'Would you come down here please?'

I went out to the landing, still in my school uniform, and was about to go downstairs when I thought of the room Swoozie used as a bedroom in the house that wasn't Mrs Overton's. I pushed the junk room door back. It was chock-a-block in there, no room to move, no bed, no dolls, games, books about fairies and ponies, and all the other cute little things Swoozie had. Welcome back to the real world, Jiggy McCue. The world of no sister and a mother who'd got this terrible thing wrong with her.

I went back to the head of the stairs and leaned

there for a minute. I didn't want to go down. As long as I stayed up here I couldn't hear the bad news. Here, there wasn't even a Swoozie to help me get through it.

'Are you coming, Jig?'

Dad's voice. He should also be at work at this time. Oh, wait. He'd said he was going to the hospital with Mum because it was such a big deal.

I went down.

'In here,' Mum said.

I went into the living room. They were sitting on the couch, very close together, holding hands. My mother and father never hold hands, so it had to be serious. I took an especially deep breath and tried to feel like a Musketeer. Bold, I mean, afraid of nothing, ready for anything. I wanted to go to Mum and give her a big hug, in spite of Rule 4. This was because I hadn't seen her for a while, you understand. The real her, I mean. I even sort of wanted to hug Dad, and that would have surprised him.

'Come and sit down, son.'

Son. My father hardly ever calls me son. When he does he's usually either fooling around or trying to play the heavy father. He didn't sound like he was trying to be heavy now, or like he was fooling.

They looked very tense sitting there. Nervous about giving me the bad news.

I was about to sit down in the chair facing the couch when I felt Swoozie's little biscuit box in my jacket pocket and remembered the effect the piece of Turkish Delight had had on Mr Rice. The Turkish Delight with the special ingredient from another world that had put such a spring in his step. Maybe, I thought, maybe if Mum was ill, the remaining piece of TD (with the second special ingredient for another world) would give her a lift too. Such a lift that she'd be cured of whatever it was she'd got. Could other-world widdle and spit be a sort of magic potion? I couldn't sure, but it was worth a try. I took the box out of my pocket.

'Before you say anything, Mum, this is for you.'

I opened the box. She looked in.

'What is it?'

'Turkish Delight.'

'Where'd you get it?'

'A friend. I've been saving it for you.'

'It looks a bit… old.'

'It's meant to look that way. It's the real stuff, authentic Delight all the way from Turkey. Eat it. Please.'

'Can I save it for later?'

'No!'

I almost shouted this. She had to have it now, before she told me what was wrong. That way she might be cured before she said it and we could all forget how close she'd come to whatever it was.

'Where did the box come from?' she asked, picking up the pink cube.

'Same friend who gave me the TD.'

I stood there while she nibbled a corner of the cube. I think she tried not to pull a face. 'The best medicine doesn't always taste nice.' She used to say that to me when I was little and screwing my face up because she was trying to get me to swallow something to get me over some illness. I didn't say it to her, though.

'Are you sure it's all right?' she said.

'Absolutely. And I'm not listening to you till you've swallowed it.'

She made a square of her lips, popped the cube in, chewed rapidly a few times, and swallowed hard. She gave a little shudder as it went down. Not a great one for sweet things, my mum. There was no immediate effect, like there'd been with Mr Rice, but maybe other-world spit took longer to do its work than other-world wee.

I put the little box away and went to the armchair. There was a pause. Mum and Dad used the pause to look at one another. I don't think I ever saw them so nervous.

'Jiggy,' Mum said eventually.

'Here,' I said. It was coming. The bad news I'd been dreading.

'Darling, you obviously suspect that something's up,' she began.

Darling. Now I knew I was in for the worst. I folded my arms so no one would see my hands shaking. Come on, Turkish Delight, do your stuff, do your stuff.

'What makes you think that?' I asked innocently.

'Well, the fact that you brought me a present, for one thing. Also, you've been so good these past few days. Tidying your room, cooking last night's meal, insisting on doing the ironing…'

'I cooked last night's meal?'

'And very good it was too.'

'Bit on the healthy side for me,' Dad muttered.

'You even stayed at home over the weekend rather than go off and enjoy yourself with your friends,' Mum said.

333

'I had a sore throat,' I reminded her.

She smiled like she knew better. But then she went all serious again.

'We can't keep it from you any longer,' she said.

I unfolded my arms and put my hands on my flat ears. 'I don't want to know.'

I saw Dad's mouth move. I took my hands away. 'What?'

'You'll have to know sooner or later,' he repeated.

'Later works for me,' I said, getting up.

'Jig.' Dad again. His stern voice. 'Your mother and I decided it would be best to keep it to ourselves until we saw the scan this afternoon. That was our deadline.'

'Deadline?' I sank back into the chair in horror.

'What your dad means,' Mum said, 'is that we planned to tell you once we knew what it was. Afraid you might take it badly, you see.'

'And now you're not?' I said.

'Now you must know. There's no way out.'

'Let me go to my room,' I pleaded.

I didn't want to hear this. Didn't want to know about it. Maybe I'd go out later, break into the school and Mr Heathcliff's broom cupboard, try and get back to Juggy's world, where his mother wasn't sick and everything was fine. Yes, I know, I wasn't thinking straight. It was a pretty sure thing that I couldn't return to Juggy's unless he was in Arnie Snit's broom cupboard at the same time, and why would he be, out of school hours – or ever again, in fact? Also, what would I do if I got through? I couldn't just waltz in and join his family? I mean, where would I *sleep*?

Mum got off the couch and came over to me. Sat on the arm of my chair. Put a hand on one of my shoulders.

'Jiggy, it's going to happen and there's nothing to be done about it,' she said. 'Now let's get it over with, shall we?'

I clenched my fists and closed my eyes. One for all and all for lunch, I thought. 'Go on then,' I said. 'If you really must.'

I heard her take a deep breath. Then she said:

'I'm going to have a baby.'

My eyes flew open. 'What!'

'I'm going to have a baby.'

'WHAT!'

'She's going to have a baby, Jig,' said Dad from the couch.

'A baby?'

'I know how hard it must be for you to accept at your age,' Mum said, 'but, well, there you are, it's a fact. An incontrovertible fact.'

'A baby?' I said, gawping up at her.

'Little human-type creature without a lot of hair,' Dad said. 'Fond of stinking the house out.'

'Yes, but... a baby?!'

'This is what we were afraid of,' Mum said.

'Afraid of?'

'That you'd take it badly.'

'I'm not taking it badly, I'm just....' I started again. 'So you're not ill.'

'Ill? Well, I wouldn't call it *ill* exactly.'

'Do you know what kind?'

'What kind?'

'Boy, girl, or alien like its parents.'

'Today's scan revealed all,' Dad said. 'Because your mum's cracking on a bit, we couldn't be certain everything would be as it should, but the scan cleared that up – she's fine – and told us what to expect.'

'And?' I said.

He looked at Mum. It was up to her to tell me. So she did.

'Jiggy, you're going to have a baby sister.'

'A sister?'

'Yes.'

'A sister?'

'Yes.'

'A sister!'

'How d'you feel about that?' Dad asked me.

I hauled myself out of the chair. I needed time to think. Solo time.

'Dunno,' I said, heading for the door.

'You're not upset?'

'Why would I be upset?'

'Well.' This was Mum. 'A boy, just into his teens, suddenly hears he's not going to be an only child any more…'

I stopped. Turned to face them.

'I promise not to be upset on one condition.'

'Condition?' said Dad.

'That you call her Suzie.'

'Suzie?'

'Suzie.'

'Why Suzie?'

I went to the door. 'I like it.'

Dad raised his eyebrows at Mum.

Mum smiled. 'Suzie's fine with me…'

Dad nodded, slowly. 'Suzie. Suzie McCue. Mm.'

'Do we have a deal?' I said.

They both looked at me. Happily. We had a deal.

'Good.'

I went out and closed the door behind me – just in time or they would have noticed the water in my eyes. I started upstairs.

Half way up, I turned and sat on the step.

Wooh.

I was going to have a baby sister.

I *am* going to have a baby sister.

A sister called Suzie.

Who's going to be the sweetest little girl you ever saw, with the biggest, bluest eyes, the spikiest hair, the nicest ways.

And because she won't be able to say Suzie exactly right when she starts to talk, she'll call herself Swoozie. Then everyone will call her that, and before you know it, it'll stick, like Jiggy has to me.

I'm going to be Swoozie McCue's big brother!

I am. I really am.

And she'll love me.

And look up to me, and not just because I'm taller than her.

And I'll watch over her while she's growing up, and read to her at bedtime, and maybe even make her bed sometimes.

And I'll tell her all the insane things that happen to me, and she'll believe me right off, without any argument, because that's the sort of person she's going to be.

And she'll call me Joseph. The only person I'll allow to do that. Everyone else – and that includes you – would still have to call me Jiggy.

Jiggy McCue

Turn the page
to find out about
Jiggy McCue's other
wildly wacky
adventures...

Something's after Jiggy McCue!
Something big and angry and invisible.
Something which hisses and flaps and stabs
his bum and generally tries to make
his life a misery. Where did it come from?

Jiggy calls together the Three Musketeers
– One for all and all for lunch! –
and they set out to send the poltergoose
back where it belongs.

Shortlisted for the Blue Peter Book Award

The underpants from hell – that's what
Jiggy calls them, and not just because they
look so gross. No, these pants are evil.
And they're in control. Of him. Of his life!
Can Jiggy get to the bottom of his
problem before it's too late?

"...the funniest book I've ever read."
Teen Titles

"Hilarious!"
The Independent

Winner of the Stockton Children's
Book of the Year Award

Feel like your life has gone down the pan?
Well here's your chance to swap it
for a better one!

When those tempting words appear on the
computer screen, Jiggy McCue just can't
resist. He hits "F for Flush" and... Oh dear.
He really shouldn't have done that. Because
the life he gets in place of his own is a very
embarrassing one – for a boy.

"Fast, furious and full of good humour."
National Literacy Association
"Altogether good fun." *School Librarian*
"Hilarity and confusion." *Teen Titles*

978 1 84121 756 7   £4.99

Jiggy McCue wants some good
luck for a change.
But instead of luck he gets a genie.
A teenage genie who turns against him.
Then the maggoty dreams start.
Dreams which, with his luck and this genie,
might just come true.

"Will have you squirming with horror and delight!"
Ottakar's 8-12 Book of the Month
"Funny, wacky and lively."
cool-reads.co.uk

When the new girl in Jiggy's class sneezes
her nose explodes. Runny nose stuff
everywhere. If you look in the runny nose
stuff you can see the future.

Pity the future is always bad.

But the little round creature from the dump
doesn't care. Future Snot is his favourite
meal. He just laps it up!

A Jiggy McCue Story

Nudie Dudie

Michael Lawrence

£4.99

978 1 84362 647 3

Jiggy McCue's clothes keep
disappearing – in public. Suddenly,
when there are teachers, friends,
neighbours and total strangers
about, he hasn't a stitch on.

What's causing this? And what can
Jiggy, Pete and Angie do to stop it?

All is revealed in Jiggy's most
embarrassing adventure yet!

When Jiggy, Pete and Angie go on the
wrong holiday, Jiggy has a feeling that
something bad is about to happen.
How right he is!
An old enemy is pulling their strings,
making them dance to his tune.

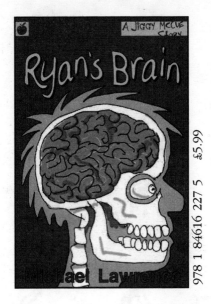

978 1 84616 227 5   £5.99

Jiggy's arch-enemy Bryan Ryan
is out to get him.
Well, his brain is: Ryan's asleep.
But the nightmare is all Jiggy's –
and Pete and Angie's of course...

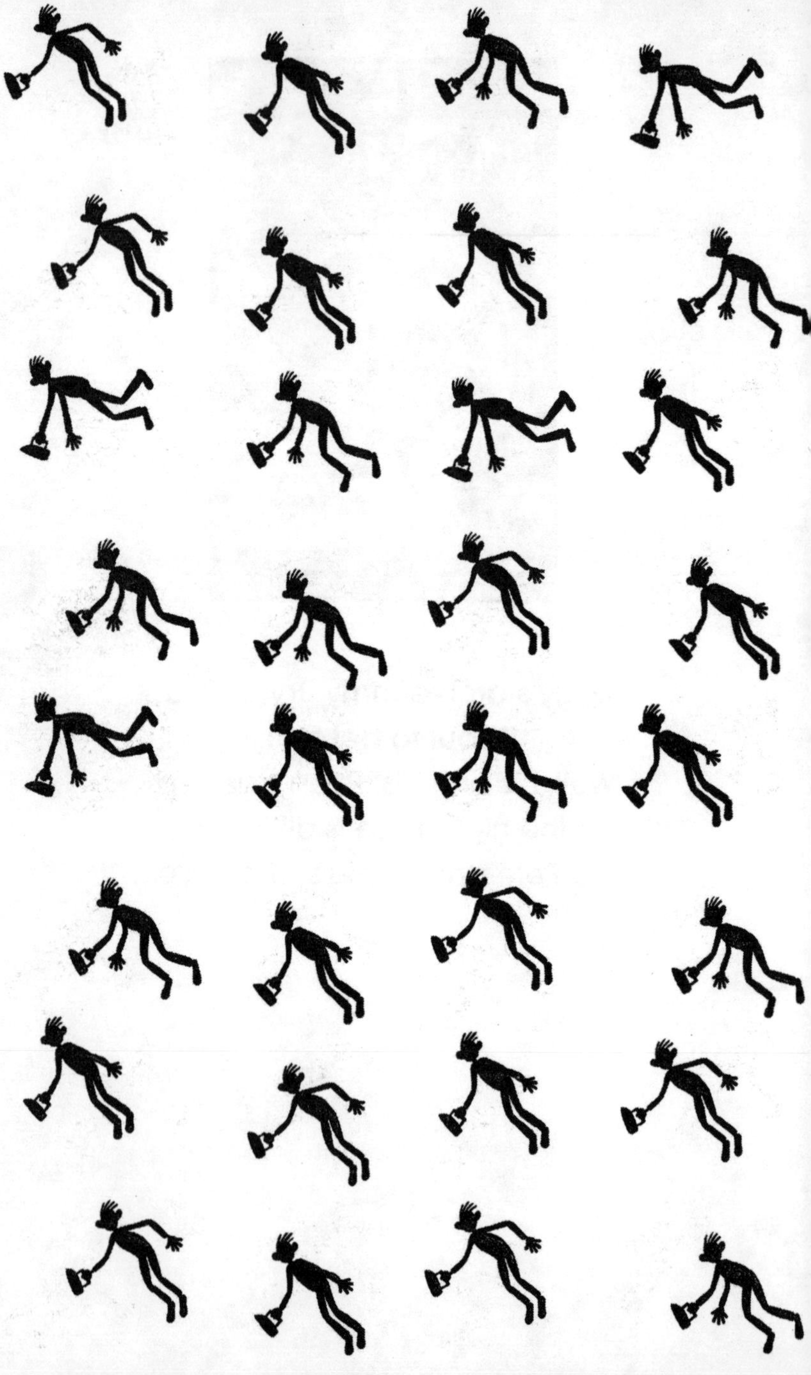

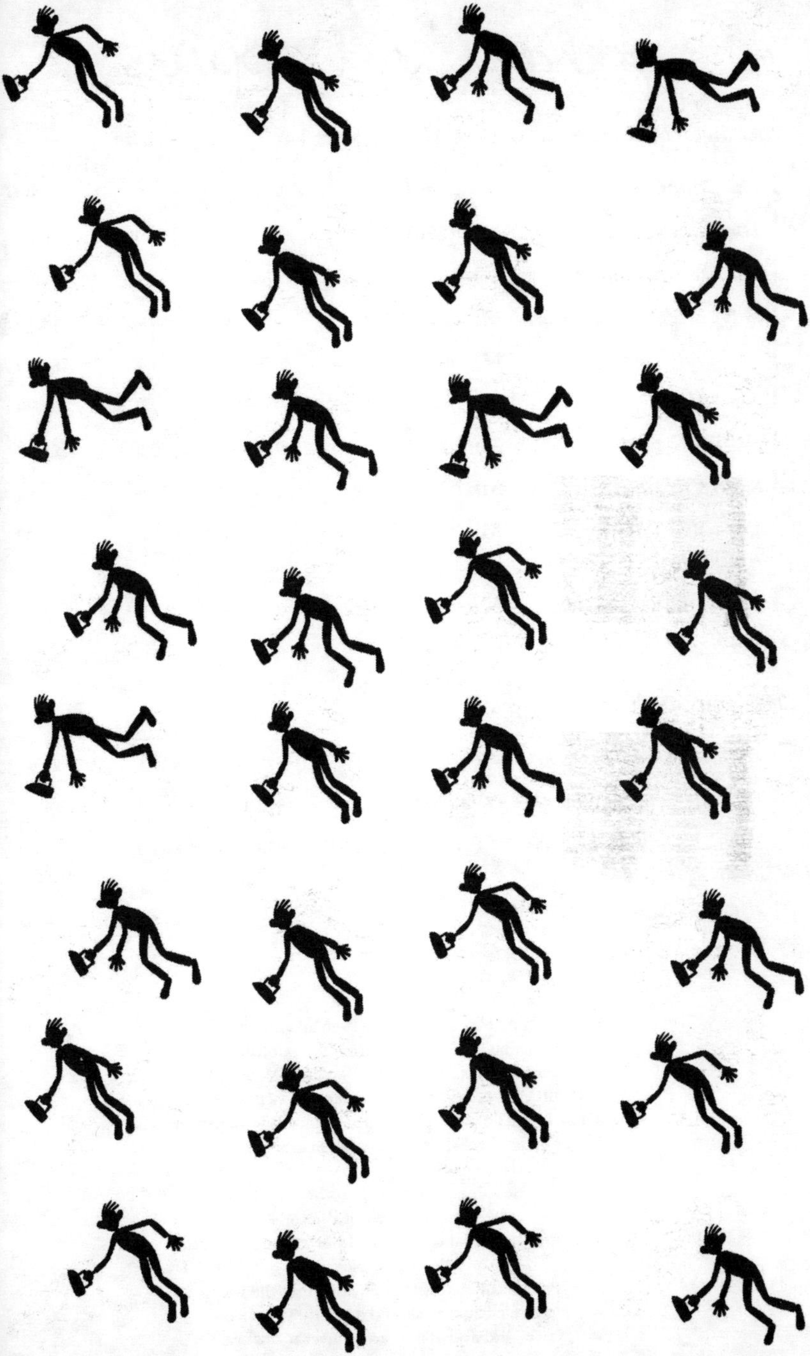

Orchard Red Apples

Other Jiggy McCue books by Michael Lawrence:

Some other Orchard Books you might enjoy:

Orchard Red Apples are available from all good bookshops,
or can be ordered direct from the publisher:
Orchard Books, PO Box 29, Douglas, IM99 1BQ
Credit card orders please telephone 01624 836000
or fax 01624 837033 or visit our Internet site: www.wattspub.co.uk
or email: bookshop@enterprise.net for details.

To order please quote title, author and ISBN
and your full name and address.
Cheques and postal orders should be made payable to
'Bookpost plc'.
Postage and packing is FREE within the UK
(overseas customers should add £1.00 per book).
Prices and availability are subject to change.